UNCOVERING HER CRAVINGS

RAE SHAWN

To the Quartet, for pushing me.

WELCOME

Sign up for my newsletter to keep up-to-date with what I'm working on.

This is the story of Leilani and Alexander. While you're here, you'll get introduced to their friends and so many others in this world.

Strap in.

Love,
   Rae Shawn

CONTENTS

PROLOGUE

LEILANI

His eyes connected with mine as his thrusts deepened. My breaths came out in shaky gasps. He shifted my ankle to his shoulder and gripped the bedrail behind my head.

"Right there," I whimpered. "Fuck. Don't stop."

When he feathered kisses along my calf, I screwed my eyes shut. Moans escaped my throat without my permission. He drilled into me like my pussy was made just for him.

"Keep your eyes on me," he said. "I need to see how I'm affecting you."

Between his comments and his movements, I was struggling to keep my focus. This shouldn't be happening... But, tonight was it. I needed a distraction. He willingly provided it.

No strings. No do-overs. A one-time deal.

I could not fuck my best friend's baby brother more than once. My fingers dug into my hair. "Oh god, oh god," I cried.

He rolled his hips into me, hitting my spot from a different angle. I needed more, so much more.

"Open your eyes, Lani," he whispered. "The way you feel, I might have to make you mine."

I couldn't listen to him anymore. He was going to have me agreeing to something I shouldn't step into. We needed to get through this so I could leave.

I reached my fingers down between us to play with my clit, but he caught my hand. My eyes peeled open. The intensity in his gaze was more than I could handle.

A sheer determination. An unfiltered desire. A carnal lust.

"Tonight, this pussy is mine," he said. "Say it."

I clamped my mouth shut. He raised an eyebrow and licked his lips, rolling his hips into me with a shocking slam that had me gasping. "You wanna play like you don't know?"

I whimpered with each deliciously punishing thrust he gave but said nothing. With the way this was going, I wouldn't be able to walk tomorrow and I wasn't really that sorry.

Yet.

He released my leg, leaning his face within inches of mine. "You've given me the silent treatment for far too long." He squeezed my side. "How long can you keep it up now, baby girl?"

Not baby girl. Anything but that. I looked away.

He took it as a challenge. His hands traveled down my sides until he slipped out of me. I went to protest. I needed to get there one more time. To forget who he was, and where I was. To fall to pieces then go home to crawl into my bed.

He flipped me on my stomach before I could register what happened. A sting heated my ass seconds after the sound of the slap dissipated.

"Ow!" I sucked in a breath as his hand soothed the spot. It felt good in the worst way. "Again. Do it again."

I climbed to all fours and pressed my ass toward him. He leaned over me, his breath ghosting a kiss against my ear. "This pussy is mine," he said. "You. Are. Mine."

He rubbed the head of his dick against my entrance. I

wiggled against him. I wanted sensations, not words. I couldn't agree to something with him. I wanted him to give me what I needed. That was all.

He chuckled and then placed soft kisses from the base of my neck to the top of my tailbone. His hands gripping and massaging in a way that had me near shaking. His hand smacked my ass in the same spot. I gasped.

"If only tonight…" he let the sentence float away between us.

Tomorrow would be a helluva fucking day. Tonight, I'd give this man what he wanted. What I wanted. What we wanted. "It's yours." I breathed.

"What was that?" He shifted on the bed behind me.

"Don't make me say it again," I pleaded.

His hands reached around either of my thighs. He pushed me to a position above what I could now see was his face between my legs. "I wanna worship every inch of you until the sun rises," he said. "Tell me it's mine."

His breath was warm against me and all I wanted was for his mouth to be on me again. *If only for tonight…*

"It's yours," I said.

"What's mine, Leilani?" he asked, the tip of his tongue flicking against my clit. I clenched to keep from falling apart. The light licks and nips were going to be the death of me.

"This pussy," I whined. "… is yours. It's yours. Tonight, I'm yours. Just fucking put your mouth on me, please."

He wasted no more time. He pulled me down on his face and ate like he wouldn't get another chance. I leaned my hands behind me, rotating my hips against his face, taking everything he was giving. Tonight, I was his. I'd worry about all of the consequences later. This was what I needed. What we needed. What we wanted.

His hand slid up my side until he reached my breast, kneading and squeezing. My hand rested over his, helping him as he continued to suck and lick, and tongue fuck the shit out of me. When our fingers pinched my nipple, I came. It was unexpected and delightfully fulfilling. He held me in place when I tried to fall to the bed beside us. "Oh god, Alex."

After a moment, he rolled us and brought his mouth back between my thighs. He worked me up until I was within an inch of my sanity. His fingers slipped inside me, curving against a spot no man had been able to find with such ease. His tongue sucked and teased my clit as he kept massaging, driving every synapse in my brain to focus on what he was doing.

My muscles tightened and I was on the verge yet again. *Fuck.* If I was going to have to remember this night for the rest of my life, I needed it to be more than worth it. Why I volunteered to take his partially tipsy ass home was the most ignorant decision I'd made in my entire life, but if this was the result, I'd live with it.

I could've been home, crying in bed. My bed. Alone. Not his, getting fucked just right. He was completely coherent when he told me what he wanted. I was the one drunk on emotion.

"Come for me, Lani," he said. "I need to taste you again."

It was my undoing. How he'd gotten me to come three times already was beyond me. But I needed his dick inside me again. I craved it more than his mouth sending me over the edge. I wasn't sure if I could last much longer, but if he wanted to show me what he could do, I needed him to give me his all. I needed this connection to rid my mind of what this weekend was and how we ended up in this bed.

"Fuck me, Alex. Fuck me like you've wanted," I moaned. "Tonight, I'm yours. This pussy is yours."

He paused before providing one final languid stroke of his tongue against me. Then he climbed up my body, kissing everywhere until he reached my lips. I hadn't let him kiss me, but the feelings in my head mixed with him pressing into me shut my mind off temporarily.

When our mouths connected, I knew this was all a huge mistake.

This meant more to him than I was willing to give. As good as he made me feel—as much as I needed this—he deserved more. All of this was wrong. He was just right, but not right for me. I wasn't for anybody. And he was my best friend's brother.

I felt a tear escape my eye as the kiss continued. This was too intimate.

"You belong with me." He whispered against my lips as he continued rocking within me, pushing my body to the top until we both fell over the edge. He breathed against my neck, placing chaste kisses along my jaw. "Be mine."

I said nothing. I couldn't. I wouldn't.

When it was all said and done, I excused myself to the bathroom. I could hear the rain falling outside louder than the spray from the shower I'd stepped into. It felt like a reflection of my emotions. I needed to stop this before it went any further. I had to leave.

Once I'd washed my body and my hair, I dressed in the PJs I'd worn over to the house in the first place and cornrowed two braids down my back. I needed my phone and my keys, which were both on the nightstand in his room.

When I walked inside, he was climbing into bed. "Lay with me."

I could hear the pleading in his tone. I should say no, but I didn't want to hurt him. Not yet. There was a soft smile on his face as I moved toward the bed. Then his phone screen lit up.

A person called Rumor was calling. Another reality crashed to the surface all too soon. He messed around a lot and all I did was add myself to his body count.

He glanced at the phone before panic coated his face in the dim moonlight. This was just another reason why I shouldn't have fallen into something with him. I grabbed my phone and keys.

"Lani, wait," he called. "It's not what you think."

It didn't matter what I thought. Fucking my best friend's brother who was barely graduating college was a bad idea. He'd fulfilled a fantasy. I'd be living a nightmare for the rest of my life.

The last thing I saw was sheer pain etched on his face as I started my car and backed out of the driveway. This was a billboard reminder not to make decisions when highly emotional.

CHAPTER ONE

LEILANI

FOUR YEARS LATER ...

The back-and-forth passive-aggressive comments that had flown across the conference room at work this afternoon played on repeat as I slid my key into the lock. The incessant bickering between managers was unnecessary.

I didn't even want to be there, but I was working on the campaign with them, so I sat quietly, hoping they wouldn't drag me into it. After an hour of their nonsense, I piped up to reel them in. It took a few hours to finally get everything fully back on track, but the day was over now.

Except, my roommate's laughter reached into the depths of the darkest part of my brain before I ever made it through the entrance to our apartment. Everything in me felt heavier as I slowly pushed the door open, silently praying they wouldn't be seated on the couch.

I loved them with all my heart, but it had been a very long day. Their high energy and ability to let things roll off them like rain wasn't something I possessed—at least not after today's drama.

My only desire for the remainder of the evening rested

on my nightstand with a, "Not now, I'm reading," bookmark on page 357 of 404, waiting patiently for me.

Between the wolf den at work and the hyena cackles coming from somewhere inside my apartment, I didn't know if I'd have the energy to look at even a single word on a page. But I'd try my damnedest. Evenings were supposed to be my time of calm, serene contentment, but today appeared to be trying my usually well-hidden patience.

Did I think my day would conclude with stealthily entering my home, tip-toeing past the fireplace, ducking behind the sectional, and crawling on my hands and knees along the breakfast nook to avoid being seen by my roommates? No, but it happened, and I couldn't begin to be mad about it.

"I'm pretty sure Lani will vehemently deny wanting to do this per usual, but it'll be fine," Missouri said. "She'll be over the moon when she takes the time to think about the news."

My eyes grew wide as I rose to my feet on the opposite side of the breakfast nook. *What the hell were they up to now?* If Missouri's aunt hadn't practically shoved this penthouse apartment down our throats, I'd have found a crappy studio to live in.

I wasn't ungrateful, I just wasn't as boisterous as they were. Funny enough, Haight-Ashbury was home to pretty much everyone we knew, and, somehow, all of us worked predominantly on Da Block, so I wouldn't be able to run too far regardless.

After verifying they hadn't seen or heard me, I padded barefoot to my bedroom. Of all of the luxuries present in the living room, the bookcase was the only one that served a regular purpose for me.

Beyond it, I lived in my room. It drove my friends wild more often than not, but they were used to it—for the most part. Closing the door with the gentlest of thuds, I walked over to my closet to use the light from within to strip out of my pantsuit and pull on a vibrant purple elephant pajama short set.

Pushing the door up to leave just enough reading light, I grabbed my book and plopped stomach down on the bed, determined to read those fifty pages tonight or raise some serious hell.

A person might think I hated books, especially given the fact that my job was to literally create and maintain promotion and marketing campaigns for them, build reader and author events, and host a calendar of twenty-seven authors, but... I loved to read.

Novels had always been my escape. My mom read diverse stories with heroines who were all shapes, colors, sizes and types of beings to me every night when I was a child. As I grew older, I started discussing those books with my father and the one friend I maintained through grade school—my absolute best friend, Christopher.

He used to get into more fights when it came to me than he did for his own affairs. The shy, chunky bookworm, with vitiligo, who kept to herself somehow managed to bother people by simply existing. It was fine.

With him, my father, and my books, I made it through—and look at me now. I lived with two beautiful and talented people who were just as much down to throw hands as Christopher had been. Sometimes, it surprised me.

A knock on my bedroom door couldn't have come at a worse time. The heroine finally had the hot sex she'd been ambling toward the entire book and was about to discover something about herself, but in barged the drop-dead gorgeous and very drunk people I called my best friends.

"I told you I smelled her perfume." Missouri sat beside my head, holding a cup of something entirely too strong for a weekday in front of my face.

"Whatever that is, no." I moved my head away from it and her.

Justice tapped my calf until I pulled myself into a cross-legged position allowing her to take the spot where my head had been. "I really would like to finish my book, ladies," I huffed.

"Get your nose out of those pages and live for a minute, Leilani," Justice said.

Rubbing my brow, I shut my eyes and took a deep breath. Only five people in the entire world had seen my attitude; my father, Christopher, these two, and Justice's younger brother.

The one I wanted to avoid at all costs after that one night. The one I occasionally thought about and wanted to kick myself over for acting on impulse instead of being the rational human I presented on most days.

When my upper lip began twitching, I felt a cold hand on my bare thigh. Opening my eyes, I saw Missouri's glitter-encrusted fingernails and brown skin.

"Don't go ballistic on us," Missouri smiled. "Justice has some good news."

"Okay." I squeezed my face before giving her my full attention. "I've had a long day. A very stressful, 'I'm sick of my job, and no matter how much I love what I do I want to quit' type of day. Please give me news that can cheer me up."

"Something exciting is going to happen soon." Justice shook with emotion.

"Are we getting concert tickets to see your boss? Because you know I love her music," I beamed. "Ooh, wait. Did your girlfriend's cousin finally put together a show so we can see him perform live? He has an amazing voice."

I snapped my fingers a couple of times. "Nope, I got it. The fine-ass singer from LA is back in town and we have front-row seats. Close enough to hump him, amirite?"

"Not even close," Missouri chuckled. "Although I'm willing to pay money to see you hump anything. I can't even recall you ever having lost your virginity."

If only they knew about the night I shared with...

"Just because you haven't seen it with your own eyes, doesn't mean it didn't happen, Zuri. I've had sex before." I rolled my eyes. "Plenty of times."

They both snickered. "Not including the reading from your books?" Justice asked.

"What the hell do you guys want?" I crossed my arms. Non-confrontational couldn't begin to describe me, except conditionally with my friends and completely when it came to the person whom I'd avoided to the best of my ability for the past damn near four years.

"Okay, okay. In all seriousness, you know I've been off and on again with Chance for more time than I'm willing to say, right?" Justice asked.

"Our ten-year reunion is in a few months, so I'd say more time than that."

"Right, which probably triggered this, but she asked me to marry her and–"

"And Justice said, 'It took you long enough.'" Missouri interrupted.

"Wait, you're getting married?" My demeanor shifted quickly.

The news couldn't be any better unless Missouri was engaged too, at which point I would expire with delight. Just because my ass planned to remain single until the end of time didn't mean that I wouldn't celebrate and be happy for everyone else. Happily ever afters' were the best kind of interruption to a shitty day.

"I'm getting married in August on our anniversary." She squealed.

Headache.

"That's six months from now..." I said. "Are you guys going to be able to get everything together by then, or are you planning on a tiny affair in a courtyard or something?"

"Lani, you know us better than that," Missouri chided. "We wouldn't let her have a backyard bash, but luckily she has a planner. All we have to do is pull together the bachelorette party. With your planning skills and my photography. We can do this."

Shuddering, I wrinkled my nose and pulled back from them. I stared between them, waiting for the laughter that told me they were joking.

"If you're making that face now, then me telling you that I want you to be my maid of honor should turn that into a smile, right?" Justice asked.

I snatched the cup of death out of Missouri's hand and downed more than half before the burn had me coughing like a chain smoker. If a bottomless pit opened up on my bedroom floor right now, I'd jump in feet first.

I pushed my fingers through the coily mess of curls atop my head, then took a deep breath working to steady myself. Ugh, I needed to straighten my hair again. So much easier to deal with, unlike the idea of helping plan a wedding. Did I even have that skill set in my repertoire? Planning, yes, but party planning? For a wedding thing?

"Oh, come on, it's not that bad. You're my best friend. Like, so is this one too, but I met you first," Justice said. "You must've known from the moment I sat next to you in orientation that this was a forever friendship. Then, we ran into Zuri during the lunch break. Sistas for life. But, by default, you have to be my maid of honor."

Missouri wasn't always who she was today. She grew up in Florida with two parents who didn't understand her nor did they care to learn. The only person she had back then who truly supported her was her younger sister, but the age difference made it hard for her to try to stand up to their parents. When Missouri came out, they told her to leave and never come back. A few years later, we met her.

Justice wasn't wrong. We have been inseparable ever since. Yet…

"I can't be your maid of honor. I don't know the first thing about weddings or,"—I waved my hand frantically before downing the rest of the contents of the cup—"The preparation for marriage stuff."

"With all the books you've read?" Justice grabbed my hand. "Come on. Plus, Missouri agrees with me. You're the only person I'd bestow those honors on. Not only because I met you first, but because the situation definitely screams your name. It would've always been you."

Damn it for being a kind person who understood emotional turmoil. I had to offer a shoulder to cry on when they needed it most, didn't I?

Justice when she was working to understand she was more into women than men, and Missouri when she fully decided to transition. Neither of them felt comfortable hiding who they truly were and I was there, holding hands and wiping noses as they worked through everything.

Sighing, I nodded my head and both of them turned into howler monkeys, causing me to fall off the bed. If the impact didn't make me dizzy, the alcohol sure as hell had.

"You could at least pretend to be happy, Leilani." Missouri scolded.

I tucked the inside of my elbow over my eyes and remained on the ground. "I am happy. I am, but damn if y'all don't be trying to bust eardrums and cause nosebleeds when you get overly excited."

Justice slapped my thigh before helping me back to the bed.

"Wait, I have to ask," Missouri said. "We aren't going to the reunion, are we?"

"Hell nah." Justice and I replied simultaneously.

The three of us hugged and laughed, and I knew finishing my book wasn't happening tonight. Those twelve pages would have to wait because these two weren't going anywhere, anytime soon.

"Fine. Okay. Be happy I love you. Let's get some of the basics out of the way," I said. "If I'm your maid of honor, has Chance chosen her—"

"Best man? She's going to do a man-of-honor," Justice said. "She wants her brother to do it, but that might not work logistically. She will ask her cousin if nothing else, but she needs to see if he can. We'll know in the next few days for sure."

"How exciting," I said. "Wait, when did you guys get engaged? The energy is here, but you already have a planner and have started working through the wedding party and everything."

I eyed her when the room fell silent. I looked toward Missouri, and she raised an eyebrow. My gaze went back to Justice.

"Umm." She wrung her fingers. "New Year's Eve."

"Bitch!" I shoved her shoulder. "That was weeks ago."

"Yeah, I chewed her out about it an hour ago. She knows better than to hide something this big from us again. But back to the wedding party, can we just acknowledge that you're going to have a hunk of man candy on your arm," Missouri said. "Which hopefully means tons of wedding hook-up vibes for you, with whoever walks with you down the aisle, or someone else."

I shook my head. If they weren't trying to get me a man or some dick, it wasn't a day that ended in 'y.'

"I love y'all, but I can't stand y'all sometimes," I laughed.

"I'm not sleeping with the man of honor or any other man attending that wedding."

They both rolled their eyes. "Okay, sure. No peer pressure," Justice said. "But speaking of behavior at the event, you do know Alex will be in the same room as us, right?"

I sighed. Of course I knew, but that didn't mean I wanted to think about it. Since his graduation, I'd been able to duck out of a room if he was in it. Work was calling. I was tired. I needed to go meet up with my dad or anything that got me out of a shared space with him.

"I'll be as nice as I can," I said. "He's the one that was always playing too much. I'm not dealing with that shit."

"It's been like a long time," Missouri said. "He's very mature and business-oriented now. I don't think he'll keep playing childish pranks on you anymore."

It wasn't the pranks I was afraid of. It was falling into bed with him again. It was remembering how good his body had made me feel. I was better than I had been then. I managed my grief differently, but that didn't mean an extended period in his presence wouldn't send my mind back to that night nor what drove us apart.

CHAPTER TWO

ALEXANDER

"THEY CAUGHT HIM AGAIN, BOSS." Barkley walked into my office as I ended a call.

I glanced up from the documents on a potential new building I'd been reading over. I took a deep breath and rested back in my chair. Barkley was the head bartender at my main club and oversaw all the training of new bar staff.

One of my bartenders had been disciplined a few times in the past for stealing. At this point, I was over it. I knew the only reason Barkley would come into my office and announce himself like that was because of that guy.

"Fourth time in a year," I sighed. "That's the LA location, right?"

He nodded. Perfect, that meant I had to hop a flight down there to take care of it before this weekend when the regular rush of clubgoers would frequent the place.

Having three spots up and running while working on establishing a fourth wasn't the easiest thing, especially when they were spread out, but even more so when people thought they could skim the register. I paid my employees generously, plus they got great tips, so I didn't understand why this man thought he should steal from me.

I'd let Barkley take care of it up until now, but that man had three strikes and was still given a final chance. At this point, ol' boy was smug about not losing his job.

"I've got it. Thanks for staying on top of this for me. You're off tomorrow for your daughter's christening, right?"

Barkley beamed. "Yup, I'm excited but nervous. Family gatherings aren't always great between my ex-girlfriend's family and mine."

"It'll be fine, I'm sure." I rose to my feet and buttoned my suit jacket. After, I walked over to clap him on the back.

He might've been older than me, but he showed so much respect. I appreciated that. Most people thought that because I was in my mid-twenties, I'd be easy to walk all over. Nothing could be further from the truth, which was why I'd go fire this ignorant ass bartender myself.

"Thanks, Alex. Everything is in order downstairs. The cash is locked up, too. I'll see you on Friday."

"See you then, B."

I went over to my desk to verify the emails I'd scheduled were indeed ready to go in the morning. After I locked up my office and went through the building—making sure everything was secure and shut down for the night—I headed home.

It wasn't that I didn't believe my staff knew what they were doing, I just tended to double-check things after the break-in two years ago. As a night owl, getting to the house when the sun was ready to open its eyes was pretty common.

Most of my work started at noon or later. With the club manager coming in on the morning shift, I could rest easy and travel around to the other locations if need be. It allowed me to sleep the morning away, blackout curtains keeping the bustling day from assaulting my senses.

What they couldn't keep from invading was my sister Justice, who had an extra key to my house. Her tiny body jumped on me at some time after nine and I wanted to chuck her on the floor.

Laughing she rolled to the bed. "Brother, how many times have you woken me up?"

"I never did it after you had a full night of work, Justice," I muttered, pulling the blanket over my head. "Didn't I say not to use my key unless it was an emergency?"

"It is an emergency, Alex." She shook my arm. "Get your little ass up."

"I'm bigger than you." Clutching the blanket tighter, I rolled over on my stomach.

"In size, Alex, but in age, I'm bigger. So do what your sister said."

Huffing, I shucked the cover away and sat back against my headboard. "Exhausted." All I needed to say.

"I know, I'll be quick. Guess what?" Justice practically started bouncing. Too tired to play this game, I stared and waited.

"Fine, you're no fun." She pouted before smile lines formed on her perfect face. "Chance asked me to marry her."

"Took y'all long enough."

"Rude." Justice shoved me and I had to catch myself on the side table to keep from falling out of bed.

"Nah, that was rude." I readjusted my body and resigned myself to not being allowed to go back to sleep.

"We're going to do it in August and we've already confirmed a few people who'll be part of the bridal party. I need to make sure you'll be there."

"Of course, Jussie. What would ever make you think I wouldn't?" My annoyance was melting away because I was genuinely happy for her.

There wasn't a chance in hell I'd miss her big day. It had

taken her long enough to come to terms with whom she liked.

"You're all big boy business now, I didn't know if you'd have time for little ol' me."

Her puppy dog eyes had me right away. I pursed my lips then shoved her and she fell on the other side of the bed laughing.

"I know there's more to it than making sure I'm coming. So, spit it out. I need a few more hours of sleep."

Justice inhaled deeply before slowly pressing it out through her pinched lips. That let me know whatever she was about to say was a bombshell.

"Well, Chance's brother is going to walk her down the aisle and she asked her cousin to be her man of honor, but he's got a lot on his plate thanks to me. I just had to open my big mouth and suggest he start his music career," she sighed. "I'm happy for him though, just makes it difficult to steal him away... sooooo."

"Sooooo, what?"

"Will you be our man of honor?"

"You want me to stand on her side? Isn't that kind of... I don't know, wrong?"

"What? No, idiass. I'd say you're on her team all the way and since I already have a maid of honor, you can't exactly stand at my side."

Even when she was a teenager, I knew she liked Chance and I wanted her to pursue her. When they broke it off the first time, I wasn't sure they'd ever find their way back to one another.

When they did, it brought me such joy. All I ever wanted was for my sister to be happy, given the rough childhood she had before our dad got remarried.

Folding my arms across my chest, I studied her face in search of manipulation. I found none.

"Who's playing that part for you?"

"It's not a casting fool," She scowled at me before tucking her feet under her and squaring her shoulders. "She is your favorite person in the whole world, though."

Pressing my back into the headboard, my mouth fell open. Of all the people she could've paired me with, it had to be the one that I secretly always wanted to be around.

The one I shared a forbidden night with the day before my graduation party years earlier. The one I wanted more than anything else. I fought against the muscles in my face, working to keep any emotion from presenting itself. It was too late, though. Justice saw through my facade.

"I figured you'd enjoy that. We're doing an engagement dinner on Saturday so everyone can get to know each other ahead of the event. Most people already know at least one other person who's in the party, but we're confirming everyone can indeed be a bridesmaid or bridesman."

"Does she know I'll be there?" I hoped she didn't hear the desperation in my voice.

Justice poked her lips out and me and lowered her eyebrows. "Duh, you're my brother."

"But does she know the role I'm playing?"

"I already told you this isn't a casting, but no. She knows you'll be at the wedding because you are family, but as far as being in the wedding party... well you just confirmed that. Nobody knows who the others are yet. Everybody will find out on Saturday."

The expression I felt mold onto my face was more than the words I could've said.

"It'll be fine," Justice said.

"She hates me," I sighed.

"No, she doesn't, she just remembers all the pranks you pulled. That's not you anymore, right?" Justice asked. "Regardless, she'll have to learn to like you because you, her, and Missouri get the honors of bachelorette party planning. And if my wedding planner backs out…"

"You'll find another one," I said.

"We'll do our best, but if push comes to shove, you and her can do it." She maneuvered her head into my line of sight. "It's a maybe, not a for sure thing. My planner just told me some stuff is going on in her personal life and she might have to back out of the agreement. If the venue is all set and everything, it'll be fine. You would do this for me, wouldn't you?"

"Oh, this is going to be a disaster before it even starts," I muttered.

She hugged me before climbing out of the bed. I watched her walk over to the door.

"I'll take that as a yes. I promise I'll try to find another planner, but given there isn't much time to get things taken care of…" Justice half-shrugged. "Go back to sleep, you can pretend this was all a dream. When you wake up again, you'll see just how wonderful this will be."

"I hate you, sister," I called after her fleeting frame.

"Love you too, brother."

How the hell she expected me to drift back into lalaland after that, I didn't know. I was honestly over the moon about her and Chance finally tying the knot.

I just didn't know how to feel about walking down an aisle with Leilani. I knew what I'd always dreamt of, but after Rumor called and Leilani thought something was happening between us, I hadn't gotten a chance to tell her what that was all about.

Yes, it was after midnight and a woman was calling my phone, but it wasn't what it seemed. Either way, things had been awkward between us at best.

Although I never said anything, I thought about it regularly. It had always been her, but she thought of me as a brat. Plain and simple. I tried to get her to see me as more, and when we shared that moment, I thought I'd broken through.

That was quickly dismissed when she ran so fast and never looked back. What was I supposed to do? What was I supposed to say? If I had mentioned it to my friends or my sister, I would've outed her, and seeing as though she did her best to avoid me on my graduation day, I knew I should just let it go.

Granted, she'd told me she likely wouldn't be at the after-party because she had a work event, but that didn't mean avoiding eye contact nor being in the photos that had been taken during the day's festivities.

I wished I'd pursued her. That I had asked her to tell me what scared her so much about having been with me. That I'd told her why a woman was calling me in the middle of the night. I knew the age difference had been a major concern, but more than that I was her best friend's brother.

I was batting from behind to begin with, and that night did more harm than good. Every other time I'd seen her, she avoided me to the best of her ability. Unfortunately, there was nothing I could say that day.

It was all about the only male in her life that mattered besides her father. I'd bribed and begged my way into an invite and it became a running joke. Justice and Missouri teased that Leilani needed a younger man in her life to show her the ropes and that I was the perfect starter kit.

Leilani needed a hero to swoop in like the men in her novels always did for the heroines. While it was jokes to them, I didn't want to be a starter, I wanted to be the one that took her off the market and brought her a happy ending.

Problem was, the more everyone joked about it, the further she ran. Even my friends took jabs. Everyone knew my pranks had transformed into a crush on the girl who'd never give me the time of day. If only they knew she worked to avoid me not because of the pranks or the teasing, but because of the night I had her in my arms.

With my sister pairing us together for this wedding, things were going to be absolutely terrible or just right. Given my track record, who knew what might happen.

CHAPTER THREE

LEILANI

DURING THE TIME I fell off the bed the other night, I must've blacked out or been too drunk to have caught the mention of Justice wanting to have dinner on Da Block so all of the bridal party could meet and get to know each other.

They made me put on the girliest outfit they could find in my closet, and had the nerve to say I needed to be on the prowl for a date—and look like I was excited to be a part of the wedding.

Don't get me wrong, my enthusiasm about the upcoming nuptials and being included knew no bounds, but I was also the biggest knot of nerves you'd ever see. The ball of twine in Kansas didn't have a damn thing on me.

The three of us and Chance were sitting at the head of the table as we waited for the other six people to arrive. I had no idea who was coming besides the obvious siblings, which I still wasn't quite ready for.

Siblings meant not only Chance's amazing brother but also Justice's annoying one, whom I'd done such a great job of avoiding. She'd never mentioned him being in the wedding party, but it only made sense for him to be a bridesman.

I could handle sitting through a dinner with him. It would be fine. I had three gorgeous women next to me and they gave me more confidence than I typically exuded. Plus, they'd made me look pretty damn amazing as well. I just had to feel that way. I preferred to be in the shadows, but with the way they'd done themselves and me up, I was a bit out of my comfort zone.

Justice's fiancée wore a skintight emerald halter dress that barely reached mid-thigh and as a model, if you took Taraji P. Henson and molded her together with Nyakim Gatwech you might reach the complexity and vision of Chance's beauty.

When she was with my best friend, they were like molten lava and Baltic amber. Speaking of Justice, she sat there in pearl hot pants with a ruby red crop top that had an intricate design of straps across her breasts displaying her skin that glowed similarly to a gemstone.

She was as tall as she was slender. Not in a bad way, though. She had more features of her dad than her mom, so her Egyptian looks faded once you got past her hair length, complexion, and eyes. The rest of her was straight-up Black American woman.

Both were sitting diagonally

in the two seats closest to me. The table was a decagon, which I didn't even know they made. I mean yeah, large circles, but not a literal table shaped to fit exactly ten people. The locations I'd yet to frequent on Divisadero Street had me shook sometimes.

Missouri's beautiful ass sat on the other side of them. She was somewhere around six feet tall. She filled out her skin in all the places a woman could imagine wanting to have body fat.

Her breasts, ample. Her hips, wide, but only enough to complement her slim waist and big behind. Her thighs, muscular, but with just enough fat on them that they gave that little jiggle.

I knew I should be completely confident in myself, but sometimes, when I stood beside my best friends, I couldn't help but compare. The fact that they all shined in something shimmery and bright, while I was in my flat-toned, floor-length, burnt orange dress should tell you exactly how our friendship worked.

Me: not flashy at all and doing everything I could to keep attention elsewhere.

Yesterday, they persuaded me to let them add strawberry blonde highlights to my chocolate brown hair. They'd straightened it and while it looked amazing, it had been a battle in itself. When they mentioned makeup today though, that was a no-go.

I only wore it when I had to attend a huge event for work, and this was not that. I'd wear it for wedding photos and the big day, but not today. Plus, this dress was already making me squirm. I mean, there were three cutouts.

One just above the small of my back and one on either side of my hips. It hung down slightly, revealing some of my vitiligo. I'd forgotten they had me buy it three years ago and I'd never put it on.

I was internally scratching my neck at the fact that they got me to put this on; damn those impulsive buys. It was better than the other option, something out of Missouri's closet that was short, skintight and shimmery like what they were wearing. That got axed really quick, like it wasn't going to happen, ever.

As people began drifting in; I saw another one of our friends from college, Alanya, a beautiful brown-skinned girl, about 5'7 and usually quieter than me, unless she was around people she liked. I wished she'd hang out with us more often, but after getting kicked out of the college, she came around occasionally, drifting a little further away as the years passed.

It made sense why, we'd graduated the year before she was supposed to. To my knowledge, no one knew the full extent of why she hadn't. Or rather, we never really talked about it.

Chance's older brother arrived not long after her. He was very good-looking, like mouthwatering "Let me suck up this drool" handsome. He was as if Tyson Beckford's smile had a baby with Idris Elba. I kept having to remind myself he was gay, though. So, no luck ever taking him for a test drive. Plus, I was trying my best to avoid the whole sleep with my friends' siblings thing.

"How's the bakery life, Alanya?" Chance asked. They were making polite small talk and I wasn't good at that one bit.

"It's pretty well. Mama Wolfe is going through her struggles but I think she'll be alright over time."

Three of the remaining four wandered in over the next ten minutes. I hadn't contributed to the conversation, nor had I fully been paying attention, but that didn't stop them or the others who sat down and immediately joined in on the discussion.

Two were fellow models and the third was one of Chance's regular photographers. It was going to be a bridal party filled with beautiful people.

Taking a deep breath, I sipped from my glass of wine and tuned into the chit-chat that was already in progress. "Well, he should be here in the next few minutes." Justice tucked her phone back in her purse. "There was an incident at work that he had to take care of, but he said he's parking now."

"Good, that way we can have proper introductions, and everyone can find out who the maid- and man-of-honor will be." Chance clasped her hands in front of her mouth. "I'm so excited. Once we get all that out of the way, we can have a lovely dinner and get to know each other more."

"Of course he would be late, though," Missouri chimed in. "He could've delegated to someone else. Almost anything that happens can be handled by one of his management staff. What's their point if he has to clean up behind them?"

My brows drew down. I worked to keep my composure. The only person I noticed missing was Alexander. Since he owned a nightclub and I heard he liked to be hands-on, that had to be who they were talking about.

"Apparently this was taken care of, including and up to every possibility that didn't lead to straight tossing the dude out," Justice shrugged. "Ol' boy had to meet the big boss because he wasn't getting the message."

I took the final contents of my cup into my mouth as his voice melted into my mind. "Hey everyone, sorry I'm late," Alexander said. "You wouldn't believe how hard some people take it when you have to fire them."

I spit out every ounce of liquid I'd been in the process of swallowing. It covered the table and the people closest to me jumped back. Half chuckled, and the others side-eyed me.

Missouri, Chance, and Justice were smiling, but trying to mask it by sipping from their glasses. Okay, so that was an accident, but damn it. I couldn't keep calm. I'd spent too many nights thinking about him again. I'd forgotten I was a thirty-two-year-old woman, not a child who could have a temper tantrum without consequence.

"Okay, thought I could do it," I said. "I adore you both, but I can't. I have to go."

Scraping my chair across the wood so I could stand, I realized my normal calm and collected demeanor was gone. And in front of people I didn't know. He made me lose all sense of rationality.

When I got to my feet, our eyes connected. He looked me

up and down, and even had the nerve to smirk. Mine, on the other hand, must have flashed the color of fire and even shown the flames because he quickly averted his gaze.

I took a deep breath, pushing it out as Justice grabbed my hand, begging me to return to my seat. Looking down, I caught sight of her pleading expression before turning to see Chance's panicked one as well. Missouri—out the corner of my eye—remained fighting her smile and sipping her wine. She loved petty and right now I was a contender for the crown.

"Please sit down, Lani," Justice whispered. "We discussed this. No teasing or joking around. He's been warned."

I shot my eyes back to him. Alexander was leaning against the door jam, one hand in his pocket, the other rubbing the stubble across his chin. The manicured curls he used to have were gone, replaced by a fade with waves deeper than the ocean.

He had one foot propped on the other and was in dress pants that hugged his thighs, a dress shirt—probably silk or something—that showed off what was definitely a very solid six-pack at this point, and a suit jacket that wrapped his arms like a gift being presented to anyone ready to unwrap him.

I rolled my tongue against the inside of my cheek. *Why was I thinking of him like that?*

Damn if he didn't look good, but I still wanted to murder him. I'd worked to prepare myself for dealing with him, but I hadn't done enough. For her wedding, I could do this. Only for her happily ever after.

But I would cut Alexander's dick off and feed it to him if he even attempted to try me. I may have been sweet, quiet, and calm, but he made my blood boil, and not in a good way.

"Fine," I said as I sat back down, and he came trotting toward the seat closest to me. "Not going to happen," I mumbled loud enough to be heard, then turned to the photographer. "Hey you, hi. I know you don't know me, but we're getting to know each other for the sake of this wedding, right? Come sit next to me."

They reluctantly plunked down in the seat after eyeing everyone around the table. Alexander was forced to sit three people down from me. My spiel only made him smirk again. Everyone took a turn going around the table, introducing themselves and telling how they knew either Chance or Justice, or in some cases both.

It came out that four people worked with one another, five went to school together and four were related in some type of way. There was some obvious overlap there. Justice, Missouri, Chance, Alanya and I all attended Frisco State.

The models had all worked with the photographer at one point or another. Chance's older brother and Justice's bratty baby one made up the final two. I struggled to keep a scowl off my face.

After we'd made it through the meal, the happy couple were giddy again and ready to announce the man- and maid-of-honor. I knew I was one of the two and I was ready to partner up with Chance's brother.

Since her cousin wasn't here, I knew it hadn't come down to that. I surprised myself and opened up a little more than I thought I would. Maybe dinner with a large crowd wasn't as bad as I imagined. Well, that was all until one of the bride's-to-be began speaking.

"I love my brother with all my heart. Because of that, he will be the man to walk me down the aisle," Chance said. "Since our father died last year, I dreaded ever getting married. Honestly, I wasn't sure if the off-and-on again with Justice would ever end, but she supported me through my difficult time. So when we decided to tie the knot, I couldn't imagine anyone else taking that step toward my honey with me. My brother has always been nothing but encouraging of everything I've ever done as well. Plus, he's fourteen years older than I am. Where else would I find me a relatively good-looking old man to make the wedding photos look great?"

The laughter was rambunctious but didn't last long. While everyone was focused on her endearing speech, I realized that if he was walking her down the aisle, he wouldn't be partnered with me. That meant...

"That spot of choosing the man of honor was bestowed upon me by my love," Justice said. "Since she stole her brother from the pot and we wanted those high honors to go to the people who have always been there for us the most..." *Oh no. Oh no. Oh no.* "I chose my little brother to be our man of honor."

The world stopped spinning. Like no air, no light, no nothing. Everything was frozen in time, even that ceased to exist. The very fabric of life itself was gone.

"I have to walk down the aisle with that little bastard?" I blurted.

"You act like you don't want to be in my presence," Alexander retorted. "You love me, just admit it and we can go on about our lives."

I looked at him, my mouth agape, before snapping it shut. "I find you appalling," I said. "Like on a chemical level."

"Well, that's rude," he said.

"It was meant to be," I said. At that point, Justice cleared her throat and I looked back at her. With another deep breath, I nodded and leaned back in my chair. "One day. Just one day to be bothered with him."

Justice and Chance glanced at each other. That told me there was another bomb they'd be dropping. Maybe not tonight, but it would be coming soon.

The mood wasn't ruined by my outbursts, most everyone found it amusing. The best friend and the kid brother arguing like family. What they didn't know was that I did despise him. I'd slipped up and let myself fall into some shit.

He'd been nothing but a menace since I met him, and I couldn't wait to go home. To do everything in my power to forget the feel of his hands on my body and the way I'd thought about it over the years.

I made eye contact with him a few times as we ate dessert. The way his gaze floated across my body reminded me of the way he'd stared at me as he ate my pussy. I couldn't look left or right without remembering how he moved inside me.

Thoughts of how he'd pranked, me and it led to everyone joking about us being an item made me want to pull my hair out. Part of those conversations had been the reason I'd tackled him into bed that night.

Fucking karma. I didn't know what I did this time, but having to be in a room longterm with him wasn't on my to-do ever again in life list. I needed to get away from him. Now.

Preparations for Monday's event at the publishing company paired with figuring out exactly what duties a maid-of-honor was supposed to perform on top of needing to deal with him was more than anybody should have to worry about at once.

Hopefully, I wouldn't have to see Alexander until right before the wedding because that would make this a helluva lot easier.

CHAPTER FOUR

ALEXANDER

LEILANI HAD ALWAYS SEEN me as the annoying kid brother of her best friend. I may have behaved that way for a few years, but honestly, I stopped being pig-headed after a while.

She was gorgeous and shy. I'd always found her fascinating. Being around her after all these years made me want to poke and prod at her until she paid me proper attention.

Was that childish? Yes. I'd need to do everything in my power not to behave as I had in the past. I thought back to all the pranks I'd pulled on her before Justice moved out of the house and stopped bringing her around regularly.

It had been loads of fun. After a certain point, I knew if I ever stood a chance of gaining her interest, I would have to stop behaving like an arrogant toddler.

That was the mind shift that had Missouri and Justice teasing me. I attempted to deter them when I started at Frisco State. I dated a couple of people here and there, but I couldn't help comparing them to Leilani—which was never a good thing. The dating spurts were part of the problem I'd had with her though.

When we had sex, I wasn't with anyone, but Rumor calling had to have made her think otherwise. I needed to explain that she was a friend, nothing more. But not until Leilani would sit down and have a conversation with me.

That would be my focus—finding a way to hang out with her well before the wedding so I could explain that everything we shared that night wasn't a fluke. That nothing was going on with anybody else. That I'd wanted her and only her since before she decided to share her body with me.

Maybe I could ask her out to dinner. We could have those conversations and hopefully, that would help her see I'd matured. Then I could invite her to the club for one of the themed nights. She'd never been there, and I wanted her to see I wasn't just a snot-nosed kid who was playing grown-up.

I was money-smart, street-smart, and I could handle anything. I wanted to talk to her after dinner the other night, but she darted out of there and I had to fly right back to Southern California.

The man down in San Diego said I'd won the bid and if I could get there before the weekend ended, everything would be mine by the beginning of March. The financing for the purchase was already in order, I'd be paying part in cash and the other part using a loan that I knew I'd be able to pay back by the end of the year.

Sunday morning, my tax attorney—who lived in Southern California—and my accountant met with me before going to speak with the building owner. We went over all of the paperwork in-depth, ensuring that it indeed would be mine and not leased from him.

Owning the pink slip on my businesses was the most important part of any of the deals I'd made over the past few years. I had to thank my father for that knowledge.

The real estate agent thought it interesting how involved

both of us wanted to be, rather than using them as the middleman to take care of everything. It assured me that out of the seven locations I'd scouted, this was the right one to go with.

To top it off, it had three levels as I wanted. The upper floor would be reserved for employee breaks, a conference room and my office for when I was in town, as well as a space for the manager I'd appoint.

The middle level would be much like a billiard hall with music and a bar, giving life to the sports theme I wanted, while the first floor would be strictly dance club style.

I liked to think of it as a twist on some of the family-friendly bar and game centers that existed, making it adult-only with games and areas they could enjoy. I considered a name for once the deal closed—The Spot, but I wasn't sure if it would stick.

Once I finally made it back home that night, I passed out, ignoring the world because the back-and-forth flights had drained all my energy. Almost two weeks passed before I heard from my sister. I knew she was knee-deep in the whole planning thing, so when she called to ask me to meet her at some event her boss had to be at most of the day, I was surprised.

Justice needed to talk to me and it couldn't wait until she was done. She wasn't the only person I wanted to speak with though. I'd finally built up the courage to ask Leilani if we could go out to eat. I was just about ready to lay my cards on the table.

After a long shower and stuffing breakfast in my face, not only did she have me drive to Nob Hill—one of the swankiest areas in Frisco—I had to be escorted to a private room in the back of the hotel. The door opened to reveal a burly woman in all black, her hair pulled into a neat, military-style bun.

"He's my brother, I need to talk to him," Justice called from behind the woman. "I'll be back in five, Renee."

Justice came shuffling out a moment later.

"I don't get to say hi to Ms. Lanai?" I teased.

"She's got to go to this announcement thing in like twenty minutes. Next time. Listen…" She leveled me with a look. This wasn't about to be playful at all. Not that I expected that since she had me drive over here. "I couldn't find another planner. I need you and Leilani to buckle down and figure out how to work together. I know you're still crushing on her. It was all over your posture during the engagement dinner."

"No." I shook my head. "That isn't a good idea. You saw how she reacted to me. We can't work together to do no wedding planning. Plus, I don't even know how to do that in the first place."

"We've already selected a venue and chosen a cake flavor. I just need you guys to go view the location and take pictures of it at night for us. We were going to go over designs with the baker in a few weeks, but we won't be able to make it for that," Justice said. "Please. I need you guys. We have a binder of pretty much everything we've been considering thanks to the person who had been planning for us. We've already practically locked in the hardest part. If we give up that date, who the hell knows when we'll be able to get that venue again."

Justice put her free hand on my shoulder and leveled me with a look, which was difficult since she was significantly shorter than me. Her other arm was occupied with a notebook and a tablet, which she pulled closer to her person. I sighed. This was the disaster I was afraid of.

"I know I can behave. I've been reminding myself how important your big day is," I said. "But, can't you just push the wedding off? Wait for your planner to get through whatever they're dealing with. Leilani and I aren't wedding planners and I don't think she'll want to deal with me on this level."

"The only reason we got our anniversary date for the wedding, which was lucky as hell, was because someone else canceled. They have a year-and-a-half-long waitlist. I'd put us on it last year when I thought I might ask Chance to marry me." Justice closed her eyes. "I know it's wrong of me to ask, but since we need a planner and an opportunity has presented itself, I figured we could kill two birds with one stone. You could use these next few months to woo Leilani like I know you want to, and we would be able to still have our wedding in August."

I stepped out of her grasp. My eyes were wide. I swallowed hard. It was one thing for me to plan to ask Leilani to dinner. It was something entirely different to spend however long it took to plan a wedding with her.

Plus, based on this conversation, it sounded like Justice hadn't told Leilani yet. *Again.* I sighed and was about to scold Justice, but then she dropped another bomb.

"Also, I haven't said anything to anyone about one other thing," she winced. "Renee wasn't sure if she wanted to hold off on doing this tour or not, but after reaching out to all the venues and securing the dates and times, it's all set now."

"Wait, hold on. You about to go on tour?"

She took a deep breath before nodding. "Surprise. But like I said it wasn't a for sure thing, but it is now. Chance and I are in a bind." Justice said. "Please. Please do this. It'll give you a shot at talking to the girl you've been crushing on. Show her who you are, not who you used to be."

"Have you talked to her about this?"

She looked toward the ground. I lifted her chin.

"Come on, sister." I got her to hold my gaze. "You talking about giving me a chance to talk to your best friend. You know damn well I'm not the one that needs convincing. I'll admit it finally. Yes, I like her. I've liked her for a long time, but… I screwed up when I was younger. If you need to work on getting someone to agree to this, it isn't me. It's Leilani. If she says yes, I'll work to be on my best behavior and get this done. But she's your friend. You need to talk to her first, not me. Family or not."

Of course I wanted to spend the next six months with Leilani, but it didn't mean I'd let my sister get me into some shit that would have Leilani's quiet, calm, relaxed ass not trying to kill us both.

Plus, Justice was unaware of the night we'd shared. While everyone assumed Leilani didn't want to be bothered with me because of the pranks, only the two of us knew the real reason why. Being nearly eight years her junior didn't help, but I knew I could prove to her I was worth it.

That started with being upfront and honest as much as I could. Wanting her from afar had been what I had to deal with over the past nearly decade and a half. Well, less than that because I didn't like her when I was a kid.

"I want to spend the next half year stuck with her," I said. "But that doesn't mean I want her to despise me and only do this because she loves you."

"She wouldn't do that though." Justice rolled her eyes. "She's supportive and there for me and Missouri, but not one thing she's done she did because she felt obligated. She wanted to. If she says no, then we'll have to push it off and that's fine. I just thought this would be an opportunity to help her along to her happily ever after as well. I know that's what you want, too."

"No, I don't," I said. "I just want her to think of me as a grown man, not a kid or a playboy."

"You don't want her long-term?" Justice raised an eyebrow. "Okay, sure. Then if I call Dad and tell him you're a bald-faced liar, you won't be upset? Even he knew you had a thing for her way back when when you were in college. He might not have said anything, but he knew. Everyone has known. It wasn't the cute crush thing either. You've wanted her. That's why you never stayed in anything longer than a few months with them other women."

I was not that easy to read. Okay, I hoped I wasn't that easy to read. If they'd known all these years, why hadn't they said something sooner? It was one thing to joke and tease, but this was an active choice to try to get me together with her best friend.

"Whatever," I said. "If Leilani agrees, then I'll do my part."

She pulled me into one of the most awkward hugs she'd ever given. "I'll tell Leilani tonight." She kissed my cheek and leaned back. "Chance will be so excited. She won't be nearly as stressed out as she was starting to get."

"We'll do—well I can't speak for Leilani—but I'll do everything I can to help Chance."

"Oh, did I forget to mention she has a couple of shoots she's going to be running through as well?"

Justice had the nerve to give me a timid, 'whoops' expression.

"That happened to slip your mind, too." I kissed her cheek and pulled out of her grasp. "If Leilani doesn't kill us all, we'll make sure all this wedding stuff comes together as y'all want. I've got a couple of things I need to take care of so that I can dedicate more focus to this in case things go positively. I'll call you later."

"Okay, I love you, brother."

"Yeah, yeah. Love you too, sister."

Justice opened the door to go back to whatever she was doing but stopped me before I got too far. "Come by Friday. If she hasn't buried our bodies somewhere, we should have all the details together by then."

"I'll bring my charm."

She made a goofy face, then disappeared into the room. Agreeing to spend an extended period with Leilani might've been a foolish choice since I couldn't figure out how to behave like a normal person whenever she was around, but this was my chance. I couldn't blow it.

If I wanted to get her to view me in any other light, that meant acting like the man everyone grew to love. As a well-respected business person who was slated to be on the top thirty under thirty, I was ready to show who I was. I wasn't some snot-nosed kid, but a successful entrepreneur and all-around loving person, who anybody would be lucky to have.

If only I wanted anybody, that would make this easier. Even trying to deny it to myself didn't work. With this gift of an opportunity, I would step out of my denial and into my truth—hopefully getting her to understand I was the one for her. Beyond the failed or purposely short relationships I'd had, I'd never seen her with a person either.

A couple of dates here and there, but neither Justice, Chance nor Missouri ever brought up someone, which let me know she hadn't found anybody outside of those books she loved to read so much. If I could be the man of her dreams, it took me pulling her out of her thoughts long enough to want me in them.

CHAPTER FIVE

LEILANI

I FELT like Justice had been walking around on eggshells for a while. I couldn't figure out what it was, but whenever I asked, she said she was sorry she hadn't told me Alexander was going to be in the wedding party.

I had been angry, but I understood. It wasn't her fault I was caught up in some feelings I didn't quite know how to digest. I didn't like him, but I'd enjoyed the sex. Missouri and Justice had no clue, and it wasn't something I ever thought I would share with them.

How could I just say, "Oh, by the way, I fucked Alexander and have been actively avoiding him ever since?"

There was no way to reveal that without it turning into a whole thing, so I vowed to keep it to myself.

It took her a while to relax her shoulders around me, but she finally did. I was surprisingly glad to see her and Missouri sitting on the couch when I got home late from a book event the publisher hosted. I was tired but wanted nothing more than to chill with my girls, which, as sad as it was to say, was rare.

"You're not going to duck into your room tonight?" Missouri teased.

"No, I'ma sit here with y'all and behave like a human," I said. "Y'all said I needed to take my nose out of my books, remember? So, what's for dinner, and what we watching?"

"Baked ziti," Justice said. "I'll make you a plate."

That was my favorite, and they only ever cooked it when it was my birthday, my mother's birthday, or when they had something they were going to say that would be a doozy.

Since the significant dates were a ways off, somebody had something to share. I looked at Missouri. She shrugged.

"I asked why she was cooking it too," she said. "She didn't tell me."

"You know I need you guys to organize the bachelorette party and a few other things, right?" Justice called from the kitchen.

"Yeah, I was going to bring that up to Missouri," I said. "You had mentioned photography. You aren't working that night. It's supposed to be fun or whatever. So, get your mind off that."

She smiled.

"I was waiting for you to catch on," she said. "I have a couple of ideas. We can discuss them later."

I nodded. Justice walked back into the living room with my plate, handing it to me before retaking her seat opposite Missouri.

"We were flipping through the channels looking for something to watch," Justice said. "Anything, in particular, you want to see?"

I cut my eyes at her after swallowing a bite. She was up to something major. They never let me pick the tv show, because they said it was always too sappy or too educational. It wasn't my fault I like the History Channel and dramatic romance flicks.

"Alright, spit it out," I said. "You've got something you're trying to butter me up for. Just tell me so I can lose my shit already."

Justice folded in on herself and sat the remote down. She looked as if she were in pain. It was worse than I could imagine. I sat my plate down.

"Damn, that bad?" Missouri asked.

Justice sucked in a deep breath before launching into a rapid-fire story.

"So, we had a wedding planner, right? But she found out her husband is sick. She didn't think it was that bad at first, but he might die. She needed to take everything off her plate that wasn't him. So, she did as much as she could before giving us the binder for the wedding." Justice paused to take a breath. "We picked out a few things already, but we aren't going to be able to get everything else ready in time unless someone takes over. I spent a few weeks trying to find another planner but no one is available right now. We're terrified of losing the date and having to wait a year plus to do everything once the dust settles."

She paused again and lifted her eyes to meet mine. *Fuck.* I hoped she wasn't thinking what I thought she was thinking. She sucked in another breath and returned to her story.

"I know Missouri has a lot going on so, I didn't think to ask her, but Leilani, you and your degree... event planning shouldn't—"

"Nope, no. absolutely not," I said. "It's one thing to plan a social media campaign, but a wedding? I don't know how to do that. No. I love you to fucking pieces, but no."

"But... I've enlisted help." Justice scooted closer to Missouri.

If not our friend, that only left one person. She was trying to put me in an early grave. I was convinced of it. That would be the only reason she'd suggest six months of her brother. I leaned forward on my elbows and dug my hands into my hair. My roots were starting to curl from the layer of sweat I'd just built up.

"He said he'd behave." Justice offered as if that were making this any easier.

"He was nothing but a menace to me for years," I said. *Then I fucked him while I was emotional.* "You think he isn't going to make the next six months hell?" *Straight through that emotional time once more.*

"I told him I needed you guys. He knows how important this is to me. To Chance," Justice said.

"I should strangle you and dump your body in the Pacific," I muttered.

"Does that mean you'll do it?" Justice asked.

"I think it means she's weighing which is the better option," Missouri chimed in.

"It's one thing to walk down the aisle with him so we make your wedding come together." I lifted my gaze to meet hers. "But, being trapped with him for half the year? Don't you know my day job is torturous enough?"

"This could allow you to branch out to other types of planning like you always wanted to do," Justice said. "I promise we tried to find another planner. We couldn't. We have a binder with everything in it. We just need a few things done. It won't take more than a meeting or two a month to get it together. Please. Please. Please."

My heart was pounding in my chest. Justice knew I wanted to eventually leave the publishing company. This would indeed give me a push to look into the other ways I could use my degree, but that didn't mean I wanted to plan a wedding, let alone with Alexander. I couldn't make a decision now. I needed some time.

"Let me think," I said. "I want to say yes because I know this is important to you and I'm so happy, but fuck if this isn't some bullshit. I know pushing the date off means next year or the following year, I'm not that unaware, but... Alexander—"

"Will be on his best behavior or I'll skin him alive," Justice said.

"I should also point out the fact that I'm pretty pissed that you asked him first." I hardened my face.

Missouri pressed herself into the cushions. She couldn't exactly move because I'd gotten a little closer to her as well. Justice scrunched her face, her teeth bared, her shoulders hiked.

"I know. I'm sorry," she said. "I asked him to come over Friday, in case you said yes. If you say no, I get it. It was kind of a dick move not to ask you first, and he chewed me out about it. If you don't want to do it, I get it. We'll just wait until it's a bit easier."

Fucking guilt train.

Intentionally or not, she said the right thing. I didn't want her to lose her date, but Alexander pointing out that she should've asked me first was what settled my mind. He put my feelings ahead of his. I'd do this, for her, but I was going to let her stew on it for a day or two.

"Fine, I'll let you know before Friday." That was it. I grabbed my plate of now lukewarm baked ziti and refocused on the TV.

It was time to figure out how to be in the same room with Alexander for long periods and not think about his dick inside me.

THE HARDEST PART about growing up in San Francisco was the fact that this place was a big city with a small-town vibe. Everybody knew everybody and nothing stayed secret.

That became the reason I didn't sleep with people from the area or even attempt to date because, by the end of the night, it was all over everywhere. How the night I'd shared with Alexander managed to avoid the gossip mill was a blessing.

I didn't understand how a place with nearly a million people managed to keep track of all the comings and goings within its forty-seven square miles. Maybe I was projecting Haight-Ashbury on every other neighborhood since the hip, upscale, tourist area definitely had everybody dipping their nose up in everybody else's business.

But that was neither here nor there. Alexander had long since opened multiple clubs and did his little dating thing. His businesses were thriving from what I'd heard, and anyone who'd ever thought we were a thing had let that ship sail. I'd fallen back into the shadows as I wanted.

It wasn't like I'd come out of them anyway, it just felt like it sometimes. Thankfully, my job didn't require people to know my face. I just had to answer emails and phone calls. I'd show up at events to make sure my contributions went well, but I was still in the wings for the most part.

If I stepped into another role as a different type of event planner or media manager, I'd be risking face time. I thought I might be able to do it. This push into the wedding planning was my chance. I'd told Justice yes on Thursday.

She squealed, then relaxed and said Chance and Alexander would meet us at the house around five o'clock on Friday. It worked for me. I'd been done with another campaign and could take a few days to figure out exactly what they needed from us.

I also spent the majority of the week wrapping my head around the fact that I was going to see Alexander regularly.

I'd pretty much settled into it by the time I picked up pizza on my way home.

When I came through the front door, that lovely little voice of his was filling the entire living room. I glanced at each of them. They were laughing and talking about something on the TV screen. I waved and headed into the dining room. They hopped up and followed me to the table.

After fifteen minutes of munching, Alexander piped up. "So, when do you guys leave?" he said.

My head snapped up. "Leave?"

"I might've left one tiny thing out." Justice pinched her fingers together. "Umm... Renee is going on tour and Chance has a few campaigns for Moves. They are opening a store in Morocco, so she's heading there for the event and the photo shoot. Then she has another in Germany, plus she has about two or three others in between and after. So, she's going to be gone for maybe three or four months."

"I'm going to kill you," I stared between the two brides-to-be.

"I didn't know she hadn't shared that bit," Chance said. "Can we not kill me?"

I glared at her for a moment before shifting my attention to Justice.

"I've already agreed to do this," I said. "You not being readily available may pose a problem, but fine. Whatever. Do know, you owe me. A lot."

"Paid trip to one of the shows overseas?" Justice tried.

"Way more than that." I finished off my slice of pizza. "Plus, we're busy planning. That wouldn't work."

I squinted my eyes. Angry didn't cover it. I was fuming, but what would I do now? Back out? No. I'd deal. It didn't change much. The room fell into silence. I leaned back in my chair. There was a binder on the table. I reached for it when

Alexander said something that had me ready to slap the dog shit out of him.

"This'll allow me the time I need to bring you out of that little cave you live in," he teased. "You have to step out of yourself to get this stuff done for them."

I slowly cut my eyes at him to catch that signature smile cross his face—the one that said he was up to something. If this was him on his best behavior, we were going to have a problem.

"I bet you I can get you out of that shell," Alexander said. "Bet I'll have you beggin' me to keep making you into a new woman."

CHAPTER SIX

ALEXANDER

"WHAT PART of 'behave how you want her to see you' didn't you get?" Justice asked.

She'd yanked me down the hall past Leilani's room. I stared at the closed door before I was basically tossed to the bed in the guest room. I pouted and readjusted to look at her.

"I'm not a little kid anymore, Jussie. You're going to have to stop treating me like one."

"Quit behaving like you are and I will." She crossed her arms. "You'll always be my younger brother. I'm here to help you grow and learn regardless of your age, ignorant ass man."

I looked toward the wall. She wasn't wrong. I was working on my big mouth, but obviously, I hadn't gotten it under control yet. Chance sat in my line of sight before turning toward Justice and shooing her from the room.

"Love you, honey," Chance said. "I'll talk to him, okay? Go finish getting packed so we can leave on time."

Once Justice departed, Chance returned her attention to me. Her sweet demeanor was there, but I could sense a deadly venom beneath it.

"You know how long it took your sister and me to settle into being together and letting the world know about it, right?"

I nodded and crossed my arms. I'd heard this speech plenty of times, I'd been the reason it was even developed, well in part anyway.

"In college, Jussie thought people wouldn't accept her because she was too femme to be lesbian or bisexual or some such nonsense. We didn't see each other for a long time before an encounter neither of us expected launched us back into each other's sphere," Chance said. "I love your sister with all of my heart and we all know these marriage situations usually happen quicker, but we decided to wait and make sure it wasn't another phase."

"I know, Chance. I'm happy for both of you. I know it means the world to truly make things official, to start your lives together and move to the next chapter, I get it."

"Then you have to know that we want you to find your happily ever after too. You've cycled through quite a number of women."

"Not that many, don't make me sound like that."

She pursed her lips. "Enough, Alex. More than enough and the reason had to be because the one you wanted the most showed no interest in you. While this is our season of love, it can be yours, too."

"What are you talking about?" I looked toward the ceiling.

"Justice told me you finally admitted to liking Leilani," she said. "Staying away from her for damn near four years did nothing to curve your arrogant and childish behaviors, nor stop the want you harbor for her. You have to completely quit all of that, and act like the man everyone else sees. You want to get her attention?"

I couldn't tell her I'd had Leilani and as soon as the deed

was done, she up and left. That she'd bolted out of my place quicker than Shelly-Ann at the sound of the start gun. That I hadn't figured out the best way to talk to her since that night. "She's Justice's friend. She'll never see me as—"

"You want her. Yes or no?"

"I do." I hunched over and started rocking my legs back and forth.

"Good, glad you're still admitting that. Now, act like the grown man you know you are," Chance said. "Highlight your assets that complement hers. Show that while you're younger than she is, it doesn't mean you can't be her other half. That you can be what she's missing and what she wants."

That was what I'd been thinking about for years. I didn't know what she liked beyond books. She hadn't been in a room with me long enough to figure out anything.

I knew I wanted to ask her to dinner, that was part of the plan. But if I couldn't keep my goofy ass mouth closed long enough to think of better conversation starters, I was losing before I could even begin.

"I know you've picked up on things," Chance said. "Think back to all of that and see what you can do to improve the areas that you screwed up before. You know she's always wanted to travel. How can you help her with that?"

My eyes twinkled at the memory of her saying how much she enjoyed beaches and staring at the expanse of the ocean. "You guys are getting married where you ran into each other and started up this whole relationship again, right?"

Chance nodded softly before pulling her legs beneath her. *Perfect.*

"Good job, that's step one. To get the ball rolling, you need to be polite and ask her out to dinner where y'all can have a good conversation. Go from there."

"Right. I have to stop the arrogance and watch my mouth.

I think she might need a breather from me though," I said. "After that, maybe I can see if she has time around any campaigns her job is doing. We can get started on this planning stuff in the next few weeks."

She stared at me and I figured it was because she wanted to see what other ideas I had. There were too many things I could do, but I shouldn't.

This needed to feel organic because if she discovered her best friend and her fiancée were helping the "kid" she couldn't stand, she might go off. The fact that I hadn't realized that was exactly what they were doing showed I wasn't thinking clearly either.

"I'll go over everything we need to plan out for you guys and make sure to leave my thick-headed personality at home," I said. "Since y'all leave tomorrow, maybe we should too. Instead of a few weeks from now, tomorrow might be better. It's her day off, isn't it?"

Chance smiled and nodded. "And you tried to say you don't pay attention to her," she teased.

I rolled my eyes and leaned back on my elbows.

"She mentioned it while we were eating," I said. "But y'all said something about having already locked in a viewing date this weekend. Y'all didn't cancel it, so we should go if it works for us. Does that mean you already have a room booked too? Maybe I could get a second room added to that booking. That's if she wants to go this weekend."

"Yup, and I've stayed at that location quite a few times in the past. I can call on your behalf and get the second room added if they have the opening. It is a weekend," Chance said. "Most importantly, don't be big-headed. While we could've pushed this off and let the date go, we thought it was past time for you and her—"

"Don't say it. Justice already gave me the spiel. Y'all trying to set us up. Leilani, from what I've seen, has never wanted a relationship. I'll see what happens and that starts with proving I'm not the kid she met all them years ago."

Even though I thought I had done that when I had her screaming my name. The shiver that rolled through me felt visible, but Chance said nothing of it.

"We'll do whatever we can to help," she smiled. "Consider this a gift to you."

We shifted the conversation to going over some of the basic things I could talk to Leilani about. We also briefly discussed some of the planning aspects.

Chance reminded me that they wanted both of their favorite cakes, but the design wasn't set in stone so they were willing to let us choose how that went. She also said we should do a cake tasting for fun before going over the design aspects with the baker.

Chance thought it was a perfect time to bond. I thought it would be torture, but we'd see. The fact that they hadn't plastered my feelings about Leilani on billboards and up and down the radio waves was nice. Everyone knew how nosey this neighborhood could be.

I didn't need anyone on the outside fucking this up before I could try. I wanted this woman. I was finally admitting that fully to myself, and two of the people I loved most in this world. I'd wanted Leilani for far too long. After the preview I'd had of her not-so-shy side, I couldn't help but lust after her more.

Thankfully, I'd spent the past two weeks focused on work. There would've been a lot on my plate otherwise. Between making sure a new person was hired in place of the one I had to fire down in LA alongside everything else, I was a little exhausted.

Balancing the workload I had with my current clubs and

what I needed to start the construction on the one down in San Diego took a lot more out of me than I expected.

But I'd got in contact with an interior decorator my sister went to school with, who's in our extended friends' circle and is a brother in my fraternity. Plus, my boy from college, whom I'd kick ass for, said he'd do the renovations for me.

CHAPTER SEVEN

LEILANI

AFTER NEARLY CHOKING Alexander when he said he'd have me begging him for anything, I went to my room. I heard either Chance or Justice swat him in the back of the head as I left. I was not here for him or that situation anymore.

It was a battle all week to prep to be around him, but knowing there wouldn't be any type of buffer was different. I needed more than a few days to wrap my brain around that.

At least for the rest of tonight, I could work on doing something that brought me peace and joy. I started back reading the book I had been trying to finish all week, but I had to put it down yet again. It was too intense.

It brought back all the feelings and love that swirled in my heart for my mother. The main character made me think of her. I didn't remember much, but I could remember how she made me feel and a few times I'd spent with her.

"YOU ARE my little piece of heaven, my gift. I was so pleased when I found out I was having you. My child," she smiled, grasping my

face in her hands. "That news was the bright moment I never thought would come. I was hurt when I was young and was told I would never have any children, but then God shined his light on me and your father, and baby girl ... you are my Doro."

When I looked at her confused, she explained.

"It means 'gift' in Greek. In school, I studied ancient civilizations. The Grecian empire, culture, architecture, and mythology were what fascinated me more than any other people living during that time." She smiled and continued even though I wasn't quite following. "I met your father right before we graduated and he made me fall in love with him, his love of words and his desire to show me a new world through writing."

My confusion never faded, but that only made her chuckle before she pulled me into a hug.

"I know you don't understand now, baby girl, but when you get older you will. Sometimes sad things happen, and usually, there's a reason for it. You are my Doro and I named you Leilani because just as you are my gift, you came from heaven to shine a light on my life and that of others. Your name means heavenly lei. You wrapped yourself around me like a beautiful necklace and gave me a truly meaningful life. Don't let anyone put your smile out, okay? Love others, baby girl, but to do that you must love yourself."

TEARS STREAKED my face as I remembered that conversation. It was two days before she died. I didn't understand most of what she was trying to tell me and was only slowly beginning to get it now. She had to have known she was dying and figured I would need answers—that I would want answers, but she couldn't have been sure how to explain any of it to me.

My mother was one-third Hawaiian and thought that, in a way, so many aspects of her life would roll back around. She'd be reincarnated as something to repay her love to those who loved her. At least that's what dad said she always thought.

Maybe she was the spirit of the books I read. Maybe she was telling me it was okay to love, to develop relationships with others. I did have three really good friends.

That had to mean I was somewhat good with building a relationship. Even though these were just friendships. Even though I was just starting to realize I'd fully let a few people in.

Even though I'd been young I saw how much she loved my father and me. How he smiled whenever she entered the room. It reminded me of the things we had planned, the things we would never get to do.

Like how she never got to teach me about managing my feelings when I started my period, or how boys would look at me differently once my breasts grew, or even how to find the perfect dress for prom. My dad had to take on all of that, and he did a great job, but it wasn't the same.

I lost so many opportunities with my mom because she was snatched away from me when I was so young. When she was so young. Only thirty-eight. I sighed and hugged the book closer to my chest. My birthday had just passed.

Her birthday had just passed. I smiled sadly as I sat on the oversized bear plush in the corner of my room. *Step out on love.* I didn't know what she meant by that, but I'd truly focus on myself and let it blossom into whatever it was supposed to.

I set the book down and wiped my face with my sleeve. I couldn't hear Alexander, Justice, or Chance, but I knew they were somewhere in the depths of the house. Maybe in her room, maybe still in the living room. It was fine. They left me alone and I needed this time to think about the circumstances I was in.

Instead of running from situations, I'd work my ass off to

face them. To speak at the moment and to get through things. I didn't want to let life keep on passing me by. Slowly, I'd step out of the shadow of myself and be the real Leilani Mitchell—the one my mother always knew I could be.

I needed to take in a different view of life... Maybe Alexander was right. Ugh. That was the last thing I ever imagined myself contemplating, but as I sat here wiping away more tears and thinking about my mother and him, I wondered if he was correct.

I would try these ignorant little dares, challenges, or whatever, and see what happened. Things had gotten out of hand before, but I couldn't blame him for that. Maybe that's what he was getting at. The fact that he knew something about me that no one else seemed to truly know.

Tackling him into his bed that night was sexually gratifying, but one of the most horrible decisions I could have made. For as long as he pined after me, giving in to my horniness and emotions opened a door. One that I was not prepared for.

Here we were, nearly four years later... My heart felt tight. I couldn't tell if it was fear of what would come next or dread from knowing I had little choice in spending a lot of time with him if I wanted to be there for my best friend.

I took a deep breath and got to my feet. No matter what happened over the next six months, I couldn't stay hiding in my room. It was time to take action because *I* wanted to not because I thought it was what someone else wanted me to do.

When I entered the hallway, I heard voices coming from the guest bedroom. I figured he was staying for the night since Justice and Chance were leaving soon.

I stopped at the open door. Chance and Alexander looked over, but before either could ask me anything—and before I lost my courage—I blurted out, "I'll take you up on that bet, kid. Just know, I won't be beggin' you for anything. Whatever little weird creepy thought ran through your head, go ahead and forget that."

His eyes roamed my body, a knowing grin plastered on his face. He leaned back on his palms. The muscles in his arms and abs highlighted themselves through the white t-shirt he had on.

That cocky little fucker. Chance clasped her hands in her lap and looked radiant as ever in her beautiful dark skin. I eyed them both suspiciously.

"No beggin' you say?" Alexander teased.

I prayed the heat of the blush I felt against my skin didn't show. Had I begged him in the past? *"This pussy... is yours. It's yours. Tonight, I'm yours. Just fucking put your mouth on me, please."* I did my best to keep a straight face. I'd mostly forgotten about that particular comment. I hoped no expression gave way to my thoughts.

When I didn't respond, he smirked. Chance looked between us but kept quiet. "Okay. Bet. Now should we lay out the ground rules?" He never let that smile drop from his lips.

"Sure." I worked to keep my straight face.

"You cut down reading to four days a week, none on weekends. All wedding planning is done with me. We go out three times a month." Alexander paused and smirked. "Can't pull you out of your shell if you stay hidden away. I think that's enough to make your head explode. Oh, but I'm entitled to add more as we go."

I flinched away and he held back a laugh as he dropped to his elbows. It made the expression all the sexier. *No sex with Alexander. Once was enough. No sex with Alexander.* Repeating the mantra didn't seem to work, so I focused on other things that annoyed me about him.

He drove me toward lunacy every chance he got. I refused

to give him a second look again. Even if it had been a handful of years, he remained much too young for me to think of him that way.

It shouldn't have happened before. It would not happen again. The intensity in his eyes told me that would be a task in and of itself.

"Fine, I can cut back on my books, but four times a week only is a no-go. It's got nothing to do with you what happens when I go to bed after a long day of wedding stuff or work," I said. "Weekends are when I'll have the most time to do the wedding crap anyway. Since we kind of have to do it together as is, makes perfect sense to kill two birds with one stone. No offense, Chance."

"None taken." She'd started grinning but remained ever the demure model.

"The going out with you three times a month thing... not going to happen."

"Okay." Alexander leaned toward me, shifting his weight to one arm. "Twice a month."

"Once a month. I already have to see you for all the wedding stuff. That'll be more than enough of your face." I raised an eyebrow.

"Fine," he said. "Let's not act like you don't enjoy looking at my face." I had the syllables on my tongue to begin my retort, but he continued speaking. "And do know, when I say go out, I mean a date."

"A what?"

That seemed to get the rise out of me he was looking for. He bit his lip and looked me up and down before that dirty smirk made a comeback. Chance brought her fist to her mouth and leaned her elbow on her leg. She was enjoying this a little too much.

The expression on her face showed pure entertainment

toward our back-and-forth verbal affair. But it wasn't anything like that for me. He was dangerously teetering on the line of letting it be known that something had happened. At least that was how it felt.

Maybe I was overreacting. Luckily, she was on the other side of him so she couldn't see any of his facial expressions.

"A. Date," he said. "One where I get to treat you to whatever I want."

"The playboy bachelor gets to treat me to whatever he wants? That sounds precarious," I scoffed. "We're doing all of this for your sister and Chance. Don't think anything more of it. I'll hang out with you once a month outside of the wedding planning, but I'm not dating you."

"I'm a grown man, Leilani," Alexander said. "Nowhere near a kid anymore, nor am I the person you're making me out to be because I had a few situationships. You should know."

My eyes went to Chance, who didn't seem to have caught on. *Did he consider me one of the girls from his past?* It was a fling. One that shouldn't be brought up again. One that I'd deeply enjoyed but long-term would be worse than eating a deep-fried Oreo every day for the rest of my life.

"Regardless, I'm not doing that anymore." He sat up as if this part was not a joke or funny to him. "I want to take you out, treat you nice and help you stop being such a stick in the mud."

I scoffed as he leaned forward placing his forearms on the tops of his thighs. His muscular thighs that I could imagine smacking against mine as he… "Chance, will you excuse us?" I asked.

"Oh, yeah. My bad." She got to her feet. At the doorway, she stopped and hugged me. "He's teasing, but don't be upset. He likes you, that's all. Maybe give him a shot."

I pulled back and looked at her, my eyes wide. She shrugged, then leaned forward and kissed my cheek. "Training wheels for a potential relationship? Maybe he'll grow out of the crush he's had on you if he gets to spend this time with you. Or..."

I shook my head and pulled out of the hug.

"Nah, no or," I whispered.

She'd spoken low so he couldn't hear her, but I felt like she'd screamed it from the mountain tops. When I glanced at Alexander, he was staring at us.

Chance sighed. "Well, thank you for agreeing to plan this for us. I know it was wrong to basically push you two into it. We did think it would be a little different. The bachelorette party was originally the plan, but... anyway, at least you have Missouri for a buffer. Justice loves you and I do too."

She squeezed me in the hug once more, then padded off down the hall toward her fiancée's room. Once it was silent again, I returned my attention to Alexander.

"So, is it still a bet? Do you think you can handle this? I dared you to do something outside of your norm, you down or nah?"

Perched against the doorframe, I folded my arms and thought about it. Could I handle being around the one person who'd seen my raw emotions and remained in my life?

One who'd experienced me uninhibited in the throes of pleasure. One who'd driven me out of my mind for the better part of the last decade. I could deal. For my best friend. For me. I could do this. I rolled my eyes, then nodded.

He bolted to his feet and clasped his hands together. "Perfect. We start tomorrow."

"What?"

My body sparked to life as he strode toward me. A tingling sensation shot straight between my thighs. The smirk on Alexander's face and the glint in his eyes, it was really real now.

I couldn't back out. I would just have to lay my own ground rules as soon as no one was in earshot of the conversation. *God, what had I gotten myself into?*

CHAPTER EIGHT

LEILANI

THE NEXT MORNING, I woke to the sound of the front door closing. As thoughts flashed through my head from the previous night, I groaned. I was meeting with Alexander at nine o'clock to head down to Oceanside so we could go check out the venue.

Justice and Chance had already booked a hotel and added a second room with a late check-in because Alex suggested we drive instead of fly. I swore he was angling to get deep under my skin. Again.

If I hadn't mentioned being off this weekend, I might've been able to get out of spending time with him, but since part of the event was already booked, I saw no reason for wasting money and time.

The quicker we got this out of the way, the quicker I could get a breather from him. I had to pull myself together and get my emotional armor ready. He could read me fairly easily and it annoyed the crap out of me. It was time to have some defenses in place.

I crawled out of bed and stretched into a big, back-bending yawn. I was so exhausted, I couldn't even pinpoint why. Okay, that was a lie. I hadn't spent any real time around Alexander since the night we had sex. My mind had been a theatre for one since I saw him at the engagement dinner.

Every single time I attempted to go to sleep, the entire affair played on repeat. I tossed and turned and woke up hoping to rid my thoughts of him, but the dream would just start from wherever it had left off when my eyes shut again. Two weeks of that could be a bit tiring.

There were wet dreams, then there were wet nightmares. No matter how good I'd felt. No matter what he'd done to my body. I couldn't let it happen again, but with the innuendo he'd been dropping into conversations, I was mentally screwed to pieces.

Today would be a long trip, but it would also be a nice firm conversation about the lack of romance the next six months would contain. Also, of how we were strictly working together to make a dream wedding happen. That was it. That was the plan. I pushed out a breath and smiled to myself.

"So, you're going like that?" Alexander asked.

I literally jumped back onto my bed at the sound of his voice. "What are you doing in my room?" I scolded.

"I called out to you a couple of times," he said. "I came in as Justice and Chance were leaving. You said to be on time for once since I didn't stay last night. So, here I am."

Looking over at the clock next to my bed, I saw that he indeed was on time. *9:01 a.m.* I groaned and looked toward the ceiling and shook my head. I realized I was in cheeky underwear and a slightly oversized shirt. I was usually up by seven, but I'd kept waking up throughout the night. *Fucking dreams.*

Of course, the one day I didn't put on full pajamas would be when he accosted me in my bedroom. Not actually accosted, but it felt that way just a little. It wasn't as if his mouth and hands hadn't been on every inch of me before, but just on principle, he needed to vacate the area. I pointed to the door, indicating I wanted him to leave. He raised an eyebrow but didn't budge.

"You do know I've seen you naked before, right?"

My eyes widened and I looked toward the wall where Missouri was likely sleeping in her room.

"She's not here either," Alexander said. "Jussie said she stayed at Tristan's for the night."

I sighed in relief.

"Okay," I said. "Well, I'm aware how much of me you've seen, but you make it sound like it was more than once."

That made him laugh. "When I stole all your clothes from the shower that one time, I kind of couldn't help getting a look at you. It was a glass door, not like it hid you or anything."

I closed my eyes and took a deep breath. I had no idea that happened. I knew my clothes had gone missing and I knew he had taken them. Not only had he been a menace, but he'd also been a damn peeping Tom.

"If you don't get your perverted ass out of my room, Alexander. I swear on everything holy—"

"Why don't you call me Alex? You've known me for what… thirteen years or something like that? It's not like you haven't said Alex bef—"

"Alexander, get out."

"You really ain't got nothing to be ashamed of," he said. "That body is what real men dream about. I know I did for many nights after—"

"Out."

He held his hands up and turned to exit, but not before adding that I had thirty minutes, or he would be barging into whatever room I was in, pulling me out of the apartment and down to his car. A groan escaped me as I flopped face down onto the bed. *And this was what I had to deal with for the next six months?*

When I finally got up a few minutes later, I walked down the hall to the bathroom I shared with Justice. My phone blasted a meditative morning podcast and I locked the door behind me. I was not about to have him bursting into any room.

I needed to hurry and wash up—regardless of his thinly veiled threat—so we could get on the road and get to the hotel. I rushed through my morning routine. The last thing I wanted was to have to deal with him for the rest of the night after we finally made it to our destination.

I was more relaxed and ready to get this show on the road by the time I'd stepped out of the shower. I had to remember I agreed to his little dare. He was hellbent on bringing me out of my so-called "shell." I was hard-pressed to show him it wasn't going to happen.

In the middle of all that, I recalled saying he could take me out once a month. Plus, the mention of that prank had reminded me that he liked to spring things on people out of nowhere, so I'd have to stay on my toes. Mentally running through my wardrobe, I knew exactly what to pack for this weekend.

I strolled down the hall back to my room—hair brushed and finally not blurry-eyed—and I found his ass waiting on my bed. Where else would he be than in my personal space? I rolled my eyes, not even acknowledging him fully. He wouldn't get the rise out of me he wanted. Not this time.

In my walk-in closet, I tossed my dirty clothes inside the basket, then grabbed a knee-length sundress with a belt and pulled it over my head. I dropped the towel after it was securely in place. He wanted to play games. Well, two could play that. *Wait, why was I entertaining his little ass?* I turned around to see him watching me, gaze intense. I cocked a hip and let my head lazily lean in the same direction.

"Can you get out?" I asked. "I'm trying to get dressed. You shouldn't be in here anyway."

He bit his lower lip and looked away, leaning back from his palms to his elbows onto the bed. The opposite direction of where he should have been going. When his tongue ran across the top one, it made me think about other places it could be. Places it had been.

Oh no. No. No. Absolutely not.

He was an annoying person who had caused me so much hell. I could not look at him like he would be a good time. *Not again. Not again. Stay on track.* I quickly turned around after I realized how badly I wanted to fuck him a second time. *Honestly, how terrible would that be? Ugh.* I kicked the closet door closed.

After pulling on a pair of lace boy shorts and grabbing a cardigan, I packed a couple of outfits for our trip, then opened the door and walked out, my backpack hanging over my shoulder. He was facing the closet, lying on my bed, propped up on his elbow. I took a breath and then walked to the door leading out of my bedroom.

"I don't appreciate you spreading your funk on my sheets," I said. "I'll have to wash when I get back. Let's go. We burning daylight."

"Oh, baby, you'll want more than my 'funk' on your sheets soon enough." The seduction in his voice was palpable. But…

"First, I'm not your anything. Second, I asked you-no, I told you to get out. Don't be a brat," I said. "Get your ass up off of my bed and get out of my room."

He looked down at the mattress and climbed to his feet. "I'm sorry," he said. "That wasn't very gentlemanly of me. I said I wouldn't be like I had been in the past. You bring out something in me. I'll do better."

That might've been a bit harsh, but damnit, my brain and body were on two different wavelengths. Dealing with him this weekend was going to be a task, and I knew he meant no harm.

I just couldn't fall into something else with him. The musk of his sandalwood cologne and a scent that was all him trailed out of the room as he left. A shiver ran through me. I sighed.

This was not one of my books. This would not end up with me falling for the one person I didn't want to be bothered with. All that time apart had done nothing for my libido.

The few one-night stands. The diving into work and ignoring any feelings he'd given my heart and my body. I was not the main character in a romance novel. I was not on the path to finding my true love.

I took one more deep breath, cleared my mind then started toward the living room before remembering to grab my phone and my charger off my nightstand. *Clear head. No distractions.* He was seated on the couch when I walked out of the hallway.

"We need to set some ground rules on top of the ones you gave me," I said. "Let's discuss this in the car."

Not five minutes later we were merging with traffic on the freeway. Only then did I remember I hadn't made my morning smoothie, so I would be starving shortly. I sighed but said nothing, stopping meant more time in the car with him and I was not here for it.

I pushed my headphones in and went back to listening to my meditation podcast. I had to figure out what the rules were. Maybe I shouldn't have announced setting some before I knew what the hell I wanted to say.

After about three hours I could no longer ignore the angry way my stomach informed me of its hunger. Nor could I start a conversation about the rules I wanted to set. This was harder than I thought. If nothing else I needed food.

Maybe that would help. Even though we'd barely made it to Paso Robles, a quaint little city in wine country, we had to stop or I would pass out.

Had we taken the more direct freeway, we'd probably be further along in the trip, but I knew he took this one because part of the time it ran along the coast. I loved the ocean. I knew what he was trying to do; to get me to talk to him.

He could try all he liked. Beyond saying I needed food, and setting whatever ground rules that would keep me from jumping him again, I didn't have plans to speak while we were in this car.

"I'm hungry."

"Your stomach has been telling me that for the past hour."

"Rude," I said. "It has not."

Alexander glanced at me, that slick smirk on his face yet again. "Yes, baby girl, it has."

"I am not your baby or your baby girl. Quit calling me that," I looked out of the window at the endless rows of grapevines and strawberry patches.

I knew the peaches and other plums were coming up soon. The smell twisted my stomach in knots. "Can we stop and grab something to eat? I didn't have breakfast."

"I would've stopped for you earlier, but you were in such a rush to get on the road," he said. "There's a bunch of great restaurants up the way, we can stop at one of them if you want."

"Sure, just get me some food, youngin'."

"I'm not all that young, baby. Don't make me have to keep reminding you that I'm a grown man now. I'm not that little eleven-year-old you met all them years ago." Alexander cut his eyes at me once more, a grin on his face. "Or the one from four years ago for that matter. I could show you if you need reminding."

"Eyes on the road, Alexander. And quit it with the baby stuff."

"Is it because baby sends your mind to a place you don't want to think about?"

Yes, that was exactly why, amongst other reasons. Yet, images of me looking over my shoulder as he pounded into me flashed through my head. I almost would've rather thought about… I blinked all of my thoughts away, shaking them from my mind with rapid speed. First rule: no mention of the sex.

None.

Not even a little.

Not going there.

"Rule number one," I said. "During this weekend and for the next six months, we will not bring up that we slept together."

"That's easy," he said. "You walked out in the middle of the night, so we didn't actually sleep together."

I could hear the pain in his voice and I should've corrected "slept together" to "had sex," but I'd bring it up again later. Instead of saying anything else, I focused instead on the beauty of this area. The sweet aroma of the fruit mixed with the salty tang of the ocean. While it had my stomach trying to uppercut me, it was also a delight.

I enjoyed this area so much. I used to come down here and pick strawberries with my parents when I was little. Damn it. If we had to stop here to eat, I could deal with him long enough to stuff my face and get back on the road.

A few days with him, that was it. Before I popped my headphone in, I heard my stomach growl and it was quite loud. He snickered but said nothing.

CHAPTER NINE

ALEXANDER

"How many in your party?" A preppy hostess asked as we stepped up to her stand in the cottage-style restaurant.

I'd come here a couple of times while scoping locations in the past. With how this particular part of California focused on wine and relaxation, I'd determined my type of club wouldn't work, but it was still beautiful nonetheless.

"Two. May we dine alfresco?" I asked, restraining myself from placing my hand on the small of Leilani's back.

I'd dreamt of holding her close to me for many nights since she'd walked out all those years ago. No matter how much this moment felt like a date, she wasn't mine. Me touching her in that possessive way wouldn't help my case. I knew she was uncomfortable with having to be with me not only this weekend but the majority of the next half year.

I would show her, to the best of my ability, that I wasn't the kid she'd met more than a decade ago. While I was younger, I could and would treat her right if she gave me a chance. Today was my first shot at doing that. We could enjoy a nice breakfast in solace or talk about the wedding. I'd let her lead the day. This was all about her comfort.

"Of course, right this way." The hostess led us through the cozy eating area—that resembled an oversized living and dining room—to a side door where the outdoor seating was located.

"Your server will be out shortly, but if I could suggest a recent favorite of mine?"

"Please do," Leilani beamed.

The hostess handed us our menus after we sat down, opening them to the meal she thought we might enjoy.

"The Æbleskiver platter is amazing. It includes the Danish pancake balls filled with whichever choice you make, two Medisterpølse, which are Danish sausages, and Æggekage, umm an egg cake that's baked."

"That sounds delicious," Leilani said. "It wasn't on the menu the last time I visited, though."

The hostess's eyes shined. "A returning guest? How lovely, well if you haven't been here since last year that would explain why. During autumn, we got a new cook. She brought some of her Nordic recipes to the board and since the owners like to have a taste of the world on the menu, they thought the new additions would work great given the proximity to some of the ingredients used," she said. "For Christmas, she made the Æbleskiver platter. It was such a huge hit that during other holiday seasons, she decided to make it as well. With Valentine's Day tomorrow, you guys got lucky coming today instead. This place will be a mess in the evening and the morning."

Oh shit. I hadn't thought about that. Leilani looked at me, but all I could do was shrug. "I'll try it out, it looks delightful," I told the hostess.

"You won't be disappointed, I promise." She grinned. "Your server is finishing up with another table, but just let her know which filling you'd like and, before you go, tell me if it was a hit or not."

I got strawberry slices for my dish and Leilani chose to one-up me and get the same thing but also add chocolate chips. The server persuaded us to get the endless blood orange mimosas because the fruit paired well with the overall meal.

The light and fluffy texture of the Æbleskiver paired with the sweet and rich flavors from both the filling and the pancake itself sent my tastebuds to another universe.

Leilani's eyes nearly rolled into the back of her head when she took a bite of her sausage and the seductive sound that came from within her had me working to focus on the food and not getting her to make that noise for me.

She'd done it before and the look of pure ecstasy now was not what she'd shown that night. This was pleasure in all sense of the word, but the way she'd arched for me and dug her nails into my back … that was—

"Alexander, try it with the Aeggkage and a piece of the Medisterpølse." Leilani talked around her hand as she continued chewing her food.

This had to mark the first time she ever showed me even a remote of kindness. I mean, on purpose that was. Now I knew I had to feed her great food to get her to speak to me. I wondered what else I could do to have a conversation. Eating wasn't the best time to talk.

When I took a bite of each different item I about died and went to heaven. I didn't know if I'd ever find something that paired this well again. The rest of breakfast went by in a blur, I remembered having two or three mimosas. I was pretty sure Leilani had just as many if not a few more.

Driving right now wasn't an option. As we left the restaurant, we thanked the hostess for her recommendation and asked where we could kill an hour or so.

"I know this is making our trip take a little longer, but I

think that food was well worth it," I said. We were on our way to a little bakery a couple of blocks away.

"Yes, and I have to say you're not so bad to be around when you aren't talking." Leilani grinned as we came to a stop at an intersection. "Now, if we could just work on your conversation skills."

"You know, if you didn't try to bite my head off every time I entered a room, maybe we'd have a chance to talk, and you'd see I'm a pretty chill guy."

"If you hadn't made it your personal mission to torture me every time you walked into a shared space, I wouldn't want to bite you."

She could always gnaw at any part of me.

"I'm pretty sure you've done exactly that already."

"Alexander." The warning in her tone seemed layered. Was she telling me to chill or that I was tempting her? Clearing my mind, I thought of something that wasn't obnoxious to say.

"How can I get you to stop thinking of me as Jussie's kid brother?"

She turned her head with what felt like deliberate slowness, then finally met my eyes. Scanning me from head to toe, Leilani licked her lips then tucked her bottom one beneath her teeth.

I took a steadying breath because if I hadn't, I might've leaned over and kissed her. Thankfully, the sound of the crosswalk system telling us to go kept either of us from doing whatever was in our heads. Before we entered the bakery, she pulled me to a stop.

"You want me to see you as a friend and not Justice's pest of a brother? Show me you deserve that upgrade. I know what happened between us, and while it was good, that doesn't mean we're friends. We were both in a vulnerable place. Prove to me that you are someone I should see as my friend instead of who I currently see you as. You and those buddies of yours aren't the best at it, but I'll consider if you make a compelling argument."

I wanted more than her friendship, but that could be a start and we could work from there. I didn't get a chance to say anything, though. Leilani entered the bakery and, good god.

I got an eyeful of her thighs as she bent over to look at the rows and rows of pastries. She tugged on the back of her dress seemingly unconsciously as she asked the person behind the counter about a few of the different baked goods.

I couldn't tear my eyes away from the soft dimples, and less pigmented curves of her legs. She couldn't know how much I loved seeing her body. Not in a sexualized way, but in the moments when she felt comfortable enough to show it. While part of my tipsy mind wanted to think about the way she felt in my arms all those years ago, this was something more.

Seeing that she'd become more comfortable in her skin since the last time I'd been around her made me happy. She was a quiet person. Not many knew she had a fire in her that was waiting to set whomever she loved ablaze.

Leilani cared more than anyone could know. I'd seen the love she'd shared not only with my sister but with Missouri. Those three were amazing. I wanted to be a part of the group Leilani had extended her heart to. As a friend, but hopefully, in due time, as her man.

Beyond her father and her best friend she'd known for damn near her entire life, I didn't know another man she wholeheartedly cared for. Well, there were the fictional ones in the books she'd always kept her nose in, but I meant living, breathing ones. I wanted to be the lucky third one she truly loved and would be there for.

That started with friendship, which meant not staring at

her thighs and wanting to nip and suck them until I reached the crease between them. *Focus, Alex.*

I came to a stop next to her and saw a box filled with six different items already. She'd already tried paying for breakfast, which wasn't going to happen on my watch. I'd have to stay out of my head about her so she couldn't sneak and buy her stuff from here.

"We can eat these over the next few days," Leilani said. "If we can't finish them, there's a place I know that will give them to the unsheltered people in the area down there."

For as quiet and shy as she came off, she was more well-traveled and versed in what's happening in our state than I thought. Most people acted as if the unhoused population didn't exist.

To know she wanted to give them a little something that could brighten their day was heartwarming. For as long as I'd known her, she'd never had to deal with not having enough. This was a side of her I wanted to know more about.

"Sounds like a plan. Get whatever you want," I placed two $20 bills on the counter. "If it's more than that let me know. We can always get a box strictly for the shelter you're talking about."

She smiled and went about picking more items. I took a seat in the far corner and watched her in amazement. Realizing there was much I didn't know about her, I hoped I'd be able to learn it soon enough.

"I know how much you love chocolate, I got you this eclair." Leilani slid the dessert in front of me before putting the two boxes of treats down. "Plus, I figured we needed to kill some time thanks to all the champagne."

"What are you gonna munch on?"

She pulled a large cupcake from within the top box, her smile barely masking her excitement. "It's a very berry twist muffin with a strawberry champagne icing."

"Didn't you say we needed to kill some time thanks to all the alcohol?"

"I'm not driving, you are. Plus, it can't possibly be that boozy. Are you saying I need to be completely sober to tolerate you and your driving? Who's your passenger, Miss Daisy?" Leilani laughed before licking icing from her index finger. "We should be further along by now, but you're acting like normal speeds are against your religion or something."

I huffed and bit into my eclair instead of responding. I should've known she couldn't avoid coming at me, even if it were a silly jab like that.

Whatever effect the mimosas had on me, it was gone now. She could be joking, but still. Maybe I was just being sensitive. "Finish your treat, Miss Daisy. We need to get a move on and you're not eating in my car."

Leilani sucked her teeth and made her way through her muffin as slowly as she possibly could. This weekend should be about us getting to know one another beyond the preconceived ideas we already had. Changing tactics might be the only way I'd make any headway with her, though.

With at least another four hours to go—based on the time of day and the route I took—if we didn't leave soon, we'd miss check-in. The one thing Chance said was not to be too late because the place was highly sought after. The staff would give the room to another waiting party if you were more than a few hours late.

CHAPTER TEN

LEILANI

ABOUT HALF-PAST SIX, we finally arrived at the hotel only to be greeted by terrible news. The two rooms Justice and Chance arranged for us were given away because we were an hour later than we said we'd be—which was more than enough apparently.

Since I wasn't confrontational normally, I held in my frustration and annoyance, but I was sure it showed on my face.

Alexander, on the other hand, was an entirely different person than I'd ever seen. The business demeanor I'd only heard about came to life before my eyes. He worked to negotiate the return of Chance's money for the deposit, but the man wasn't very willing to budge.

It took about twenty minutes before he got the man to agree to return half of the money. It was only really due to the legalese Alexander spewed about timeframes and inconveniences. I figured it was because the manager didn't want to be too much of an ass during the Valentine's Day weekend.

I didn't know he had it in him to be so put together. It

was my fault we were late though. First, we stopped to eat, then we stopped to fill up the tank and drop off the extra box of donuts I'd gotten for the shelter. We likely would've been on time had I not meandered.

But nonetheless, hotels in the area were full. Luckily, I knew someone who lived not far from the venue—my best guy friend. Soon we were pulling up to his house. The kid who'd had always been like a brother was far from that now.

Christopher was grown with a wife and children of his own, and I appreciated him all the same. He'd always supported and helped me out when I truly needed it. Which, in this case, meant lending us his back house.

"Thank you, Chris, like so much. You don't even know what this means to me."

Christopher pulled me into one of the tight hugs he used to give me when we were younger, the type a person had to squeeze out of before they popped. When I could finally breathe again, I turned to see his very pregnant wife. Her glow was more than evident and highlighted how drop-dead gorgeous she was. They'd just stepped out of his SUV in the driveway when we'd pulled up.

"Hey, baby girl," Christopher said. "It's good to finally see you again. Nice to see you too, little Alex. You're not so little anymore, though."

Alexander hugged him and patted him on the back. "What was that? Your wedding, right?" Alexander asked.

"Yup, I remember you and your sister coming to that," Christopher said. "That was three years after—"

I maneuvered around the two of them so they could do their little catch-up while I walked over to my sister-in-law, for all intents and purposes.

"Mercedes," I squealed. "You're getting along there, aren't you?"

She rubbed her stomach before pulling me to her in an

awkward around-her-belly embrace. Thankfully, it was less bear hug-worthy than what Christopher had given.

"Lani, honey, we missed you so much. You really need to come down more often, but yes. Two more months and I'll be ready to take this bun out the oven. Speaking of, when are we ever going to get a niece or nephew from you?"

"Don't wish that on me. You know I'm not the mother type. I'll be God mommy to your kids and love them like my own, but none will be popping out of here."

Christopher and Alexander walked up beside us, shaking their heads. I ignored it. Christopher wanted me to find someone to bring me "to the light" for more than a decade.

I remembered almost spilling the beans to them about whom I'd slept with that night all those years ago, but I'd kept it to myself. Alexander was just the annoying little brother of my best friend.

While Christopher didn't know Justice and Missouri that well, he would have found a way to join their team and push me even more toward finding love. If that happened to be with my friend's little brother, Christopher wouldn't have cared.

As far as kids went, there would be none of that. Alexander wanted a niece or nephew, but Justice said neither she nor Chance wanted to go through IVF, and adoption plans weren't on their agenda for at least another decade, so he had a while to wait. Missouri didn't want children yet either, so that left me. Problem was, I didn't want little ones at all.

"So, anyway, Alex, how are the nightclubs coming along?" Christopher asked. "I remember you saying you were going to be this big ol' successful business owner. I kept my eyes peeled. Heard you were opening one in San Diego. That's your, what? Fourth?"

"Yeah, man. I just came from down here not too long ago.

Finalized everything and got a good friend helping smooth out the construction side of things," Alexander said. "I'm just lucky my dad was able to help me with the initial club; it would've been damn near impossible to get this far without his support."

We'd walked into the house at that point and were settling onto the couch as their two children came waddle-running into the room, their babysitter not far off.

"Sorry, Mr. and Mrs. White. They heard you guys come in. They dropped all of their toys and took off in here." The young girl, probably no more than nineteen, said.

"No worries, you can head out. We are in for the evening. Again, thank you so much, and tell your sister we said hi." Mercedes said after paying her.

"You know my back house is a one-bedroom set up, like a studio, right?" Christopher said. "I mean, it has an area for cooking and a small bathroom with a shower, but it's what we use when we're working from home so it's not much."

Alexander and I exchanged glances.

"It's better than sleeping in the car," he said. "We'll make it work."

Great. As if his body pressed up against mine hadn't been a thought already. *Get it together, girl.* After a short conversation with them, Alexander and I double-checked with the venue to make sure we could still come tonight.

Since the wedding reception was supposed to be in the evening, we'd asked if we could view the space after sundown. They'd happily pushed the walkthrough back a few hours, which was probably the best news we'd gotten all day.

When we arrived, the temperature had dropped what felt like ten degrees. Thankfully, I'd been cognizant enough to grab a thicker sweater this morning.

"You warm enough to walk around for this?" Alexander asked once we'd parked.

"We are already here," I said. "I'll survive. I should've thought about my choice of outfit a bit more, but we'll be indoors part of the time."

"I have an extra coat in the back if you're still chilly. Just let me know." I glanced at his attire.

When he'd walked into the restaurant a few weeks back, he was in a suit. When I saw him yesterday, he was in a suit. Today, he had on jeans and a dress shirt. Alexander stepped out of the car and popped open the back door to grab a coat from the backseat.

He rubbed his palms together before blowing on them, then pulled on the blazer. If nothing else, the man knew how to wear something that complimented every inch of him.

I smiled to myself and shook my head. My mind was going to be the death of me. Yes, he was a grown man, but looking at him in that light would allow my mind to wander to places it shouldn't. Alexander was still Justice's little brother—who I'd had sex with—regardless of the crush Chance apparently knew of. That was all the more reason not to add fuel to the flame.

I could do this. I could make it through this weekend and the next six months. When I turned to my door, Alexander was there pulling it open for me.

The venue was phenomenal. Justice and Chance had chosen an amazing space. The events manager showed us different ways it had been used in the past. We got to talk about how the lighting could be set up, where the reception would be exactly, and how chairs could be aligned differently in the space.

It was kind of invigorating to think about planning in this way. I thought I'd dread it more, but I loved it. But after a little more than an hour, I was freezing even though Alex had given me his blazer and went back out to the car to grab his coat about halfway through the time we were there.

By nine o'clock we were sitting at the dinner table with Christopher and Mercedes—happy to be out of the chilly weather and ready to eat. Alexander's scent was still invading my nostrils, even though I'd taken his blazer off. I worked extra hard to focus on the food rather than the way his clothing had made my mind wander.

Christopher and Mercedes had already eaten with the kids by the time we'd gotten back, but they made us plates and decided to help us come up with ideas for the bachelorette party. I mentioned a few of the suggestions Missouri and I had discussed earlier in the week, but none of us were completely sold on them.

"What if we like rent a hotel or something and order them strippers?" I tossed out before eating my last forkful of salad. I'd almost forgotten Chris and Mercedes were vegetarian, but their meals were always filling and hearty as hell.

The roasted pumpkin with lentils, tahini, and za'atar hit the spot more than I'd expected, more than the delicious brunch we'd had on the road—which was by far amazing beyond belief. With all the stuff I'd packed in today, I wanted nothing more than to finish this conversation so I could pass out.

"That's so cliché," Alexander teased. "Do better."

I wanted to punch him.

"What about that party bus idea you said Missouri mentioned? How about adding a twist to that? You could travel to a few places and get drunk in your own comforts," Mercedes said. "Make it like a bar hop party bus ride."

"Actually, that does sound perfect," Christopher added. "I've only met Justice a couple of times, but it seems her speed."

"Her fiancée would love that," Alexander admitted.

"Great. Okay. Sure. Party bus. Bars. We can start looking into that." Everything came out in a mumble. I didn't like partying, especially when flitting from bar to bar like that, but this was about them and I knew they'd love it.

"I'm kind of exhausted from the drive and everything, so I'm going to head over to take a shower and get some sleep." I stood to go wash my dish. "Again, thank you guys for letting us stay here."

"Leave the plate, Lani." Christopher took it from me. "You're a guest. Just let me know if you guys need anything."

I gave him a quick hug and kissed Mercedes' cheek before dipping out to the back house, if you could even call it that. It really was small. More like an oversized shed—a luxurious one with super fancy furniture and bedding, but a shed nonetheless.

The problem with it was that it looked like a tiny studio apartment. Everything was scattered around the singular room. A kitchenette in the far-left corner, a bed against the far-right wall, the bathroom a hop, skip and a jump from the left side of the bed, then there was a desk and chair near the door and a loveseat across from it, just off the front of the bed.

Thank goodness. He could sleep on the couch.

After I got out of the shower and dressed in the cute pajama set I'd brought, I walked out to see my annoying gnat passed out across the mattress. *Oh no the hell he didn't.* But damn if his sleeping figure didn't look even more appealing than I'd imagined.

The way Alexander's lips parted just barely. The look of utter relaxation across his face. The way he cradled the pillow. He looked much more a man than he did four years ago. I sighed. As much as I should let him sleep. I wouldn't be able to rest if he were in the bed that close to me.

"Alexander." No response.

"Alexander." Still nothing.

"Boy, if you don't wake your big ass up." I started shaking his shoulder. "Alexander... Alex."

He reached up and pulled me down against him, his face centimeters from mine.

"Will you stop?" He mumbled, his breath kissing me almost as much as the accidental pressure from his lips as he spoke. "I'm trying to sleep."

I squirmed until he let me go. Alexander's eyes slowly opened, and a smile crawled across his lips. "Sorry, but damn. You felt good in my arms. Don't you want to come back?"

I chucked a pillow at him, wide-eyed. "No, go sleep on the couch. I'm not sharing a bed with you."

"You almost did before," he said. "So, I'd say, 'Not yet you aren't.'"

"Not then. Not now. Not ever," I said. "And remember rule number one?"

"I do, but as I said earlier, we didn't sleep together, so I'm not breaking the rule," he said. "Also, you called me Alex. There's another thing you said you'd never do."

Damn it, I did. "Couch."

He sat up and gently grabbed my arm, pulling me toward him. My heart rate spiked, but I didn't stop nor lean away because I wanted to see what he'd do. *What has gotten into me?* I wasn't sure, but it was in charge of my body and mind at the moment. As Alexander's fingers danced up the back of my arm, I felt fire in their wake.

My lips parted and I sucked in a breath. I saw his eyes drop to my mouth. An intensity in them that made my stomach flip. He swallowed hard enough that I saw his Adam's apple bobble. Then he brought me even closer to him.

My chest ached because he was prolonging this. Why

couldn't he just kiss me already? Why did I want him to? *Fuck it and the warning sign flashing at me.* I was breaking my own damn rules before I could even lay them out.

Snapping forward, I pushed Alexander down on the bed and climbed over him. My lips met his. He froze for all of two seconds before his fingers dug into my hair and held me in place as his other hand slid beneath my shorts, grabbing my bare ass cheek.

I bit his lower lip, growling in frustration as I realized I'd kissed him and not the other way around. It didn't matter, I wanted his mouth on mine. And here we were. The grin on his face as he rubbed his tongue against mine sent pools of desire into my groin. I couldn't fuck him. I couldn't. This had to stop. Yet…

When he flipped us so he was on top, I knew things were about to escalate. Him spreading my thighs with his knees. His dick pressed against me through the thin fabric. A moan I didn't intend to make slipped from my lips. I held my breath.

This couldn't be happening right now. My hands clawed at his shirt, angling to get it off of him. He leaned back, leaving me a puddle of want, and yanked it over his head. The body that had been on my mind since he walked into the restaurant looked good enough to eat.

Even better than the last time I'd seen it.

Fragments of thoughts flashed through my mind. A bite here. A lick there. Rubbing my hand down his chest as he… I sucked in a breath, putting my hand against his taunt abs before he could return to me. Tilting his head to the side, he leaned back on his haunches.

"W-we shouldn't do this," I panted. "Couch. Sleep on the couch, Alexander."

But before he could move away, I reached up and pulled him back to my lips. My legs wrapped around his back. He pushed my shirt up my sides, leaning back just enough to help me out of it before his mouth recaptured mines. I froze when he shifted to my neck, his teeth dragging along my pulse.

"No, wait. Seriously, we shouldn't." I closed my eyes and covered my face. "Go. Now."

"You sure because if I go to move again and you pull me back, it's going to be difficult to stop myself from feeling a little bit smug."

"No, I'm not sure. I mean... yes. Go. Get."

Peaking from between my fingers, I saw Alexander's smile. He didn't say another word. Instead, he nodded, grabbed a pillow and blanket from beside my head, kissed my temple, then took the bedding over to the couch where he promptly laid down.

No, wait. I wanted this. Just this once. If I got it this once, I could set the ground rules after this. If I didn't rectify my desires now, I wouldn't be able to focus moving forward. I sucked in a deep breath before climbing out of the bed.

CHAPTER ELEVEN

ALEXANDER

Fuck. Having Leilani's lips on mine again...

I squeezed my eyes shut tightly. This trip wasn't about that. I was supposed to show her I was worthy of friendship and maybe more. Stimulating her body was something I knew I could do. I needed to arouse her mind.

I pulled the cover over my shoulder and worked to get comfortable on the couch. I heard the bed shift behind me. I worked to flush the thoughts of her half-naked body from the darkness of my thoughts.

Sports. Building permits. New drink menus. Hiring new staff. Anything to keep me from drifting back to the soft gasps she'd let out moments ago.

"Alexander," Leilani said.

I fluttered my eyes open to see her still half-naked and standing right before me. Her breasts remained bare. I double-blinked, thinking I'd conjured her in my half-sleep mind. She reached a hand out to me. I shucked the blanket to the side and sat up.

"Lani?" I asked, slowly taking her hand.

"My mind won't stop reminding me of that night, and I'm

sure yours hasn't let you rest either," Leilani said. "I was going to make a no-sex rule, but given where my mind is right now, I don't think that would have lasted. The fact that it hasn't even been a full day…"

She groaned and sat beside me. I followed her movements, still wondering if this was a fever dream. Had I even awoken or was I still passed out in bed?

"I have three rules and if you agree, I think we should get this out of our system," Leilani said. "I'll tell you what they are. We'll go from there. If you answer no to any of them, I understand."

I swallowed and nodded my head. I couldn't get words to leave my throat even if I wanted them to. I couldn't fully understand what was happening right now. I mean I could, she was setting ground rules, but I hadn't imagined this.

"First rule, no kissing. It's too intimate," Leilani said. "I know we've kissed before and it's part of what scares me about this. So, your lips can be anywhere on my body, but my mouth. Agreed?"

I felt my dick getting hard. Just knowing she wanted me to touch her with my mouth again. It wasn't one-sided. It was something she'd carefully ignored all this time. I slowly nodded.

"Okay. Good. Second rule, if things happen again. We go with the flow, but only during and up to the day of the wedding," she said. "This ends by then."

Hold the hell up? Was she saying…?

"Yes, based on the face you're making, you're wondering if I'm saying will this last beyond tonight." Leilani smiled. "As much as the back of my mind is screaming how bad of an idea this could be. I think we both need to take the time to see that this is nothing more than sexual compatibility. One time isn't going to be enough, no matter how much I want to tell myself it would be."

I didn't know how I could explain that to her, but this was more than a physical thing for me. If Leilani was allowing six months to have her in my arms, maybe I could figure out a way to convince her to stay.

I wasn't just a bratty kid. I was a man whom she could love and trust. Who was worthy of being beside her. Whom she could be shy and quiet or loud and boisterous with. I was for her. I was the hero in the story and she was the heroine I'd dreamt of for years.

"Cool. Two for two. So, rule number three, we do not tell anyone about this," Leilani said. "Not your two knuckleheaded friends. Not mine either. It stays between us."

"Understood," I said.

That I didn't mind. If anyone started saying something, it would only put her in her head and she'd pull back from me. If we were going to share this with anyone, it would have to be after we actually decided to make it official. Otherwise, it would be blown out of proportion. So, just us for now.

She leaned forward and kissed my cheek before climbing into my lap. "Okay, Mr. Rutherford. You're fine with my rules, and I'm fine with yours. To say you've pulled me out of my shell already is kind of annoying, but I'll admit it, at least for now."

I smiled and kept myself from brushing my lips across hers. Not being able to taste her lips again would be the most difficult, but I would do my best.

"So, what now?" I asked.

"How about we pick up where we left off?" Leilani climbed from my lap and pulled me to a stand. We walked over to the bed and she stopped short. I caught her around her waist when she rocked forward from me bumping into her.

"Careful, sweetheart," I said.

After hearing Chris call her baby girl, I understood that

was a nickname he'd given her. I wouldn't use it or baby moving forward. I could understand how that would feel awkward or even uncomfortable.

Leilani reached an arm behind her and placed it on my shoulder, tilting her head to the side. I dropped feather-like kisses from the edge of her shoulder to just beneath her earlobe. *Fuck*. My dick was about to be angry as hell with me.

"I don't have condoms," I groaned.

She peeled her body from mines, turning in my grasp until her arms were draped around my neck.

"Good thing I came prepared," she said.

I blinked absently at her. Had I been reading her wrong this entire time? A smirk appeared on her face.

"While Justice and Missouri are adamant that I haven't had sex. You, for one, can attest that I have." Leilani reached up on her tiptoes to kiss my chin. "I keep one on me in case a situation happens."

"May I ask when was the last time a situation happened?"

"Today," she smirked.

Okay, she wasn't going to tell me. I respected that. Privacy through and through.

"Where's the condom?" I asked.

She melted down to her knees in front of me. I had to take a step back or my dick would've put her eye out. It was pressed firmly against the seam of my jeans, begging to be released. She grinned and grabbed her bag from under the bed. After fishing it out, she tossed it on the sheets and reached for the button on my pants.

My hands covered hers. As much as I'd love to have Leilani's mouth wrapped around my dick, I thought I should shower away the day before this went any further. The tease in the bed earlier was because I figured she wouldn't let it go anywhere. Never had I imagined we'd be where we are now.

"Let me start by saying, I want this more than you could

know, but I should shower like you did," I groaned hearing the words leave my mouth. "I promise I'm not—"

She rose to her feet and walked into the bathroom without a word. I heard the shower turn on moments later. I cocked my head but didn't walk over.

"You coming or not?" Leilani called. "If you are, bring the condom. If not, I'll use this showerhead."

I huffed but left the condom where it was. Get my body clean. Eat her out in the shower and finish in bed. *Priorities.* After quickly stripping out of my jeans and boxer briefs, I entered the small bathroom.

Leilani was standing naked under the spray, her back to me. I could see every single piece of her and I felt my dick jump. I'd damn near prayed for another chance to have her naked in front of me.

The shower was small, barely large enough to fit us, and the built-in seat that likely was for Mercedes since she was pregnant. I could sit Leilani on that and kneel before her to suck and lick every inch of her… or I could save that for the bed where I'd have much more space. *Adjusted priorities.*

I opened the door and stepped in behind her. She turned toward me, a lust in her eyes I hadn't seen since that night. This wasn't a fluke. It wasn't a dream. Leilani truly wanted me and I could have her as long as I didn't fuck up her rules. It was limited time, but damn it I'd make plans to show her I could be the love interest in her story.

She grabbed the bar of soap and lathered the hand towel. "One can never be too clean, but how about we get you good and ready, so we can… get to it."

If showering had ever been thought of as foreplay before, I didn't know, but Leilani had only made me want to sink into her all the more. The way she rubbed her hands across my body, the towel a thin veil between us. The intensity in her eyes. After a few moments, she smirked and left me to focus on my skin while she washed her hair. I figured it was only so she could stay close to me.

My skin heated with every brush of hers across mine. I needed to get her from under this spray, now. I helped her rinse the soap from her hair. She assured me there was none left on my body after I spun around a few times. Once she'd had her fill of teasing, I quickly got us from that shower to the bed.

Leilani giggled when we fell to the mattress. The towel she'd tied her hair up in unraveled as soon as we landed. "Now that we're both clean…"

She rolled atop me and planted soft kisses down my chest. I dropped my head back on the pillow before lifting it to watch her work down my body. Her hands smoothed to the top of my towel, pulling it apart just before her lips reached my waist. My stomach clenched. She smirked. Leilani might be quiet, but she damn sure knew what she wanted.

She sat up on her knees and looked down at my dick before licking her lips. Slowly her hand enveloped me, gripping with just enough pressure to elicit a moan. Her eyes snapped to mine. My hands were languid at my sides, but I had a feeling that was about to change.

She lowered her mouth to me until the tip of her tongue could swirl around the head of my dick. "Oh, fuck." I breathed. Leilani was going to torture me sweetly, gingerly. She covered me inch by inch, the warmth of her mouth sending my good sense elsewhere.

She kept her hand at the base of my dick and when she lifted her mouth, her fingers moved along with it. Leilani softly twisted and squeezed, raising and lowering her head until she found a rhythm that had my toes curling and my hands balling in the sheets. *What the hell was she doing to me?*

The way her tongue swirled as her hand fucked me just

as good as her mouth had me making sounds I didn't know I could. She moaned against me. I felt the vibration from the back of her throat on the head of my dick and nearly lost it.

My stomach tensed, and I felt the pressure in my balls building up. As if she knew I was almost there, she began massaging my sack. I sat up on my elbows and watched her the best I could. Her eyes connected with mine—all shyness and innocence gone. I tangled my hand in her hair and continued to watch her.

Leilani sped up and twisted her mouth and hand against me one, two, three more times before I pulled her off and shot my load into the towel. My breaths were ragged. It was one thing to feel her mouth on me, but to watch her doing it… that sent my body to another level.

"I wanted to taste you," Leilani said, a seduction in her voice I hadn't heard in way too long. I might not be able to fuck her like I wanted to yet, but I damn sure could reciprocate this feeling.

"Next time," I managed. After ensuring I was done with the after-shocks, I tossed the towel on the ground and slowly prowled over to her at the edge of the bed. "Didn't mean to yank your hair like that."

"Maybe next time you'll do it a little rougher," Leilani said. "I'm not as fragile as I appear. You should remember how much of a pretzel you tried to make me last time."

Visions of her legs on my shoulders and the bed rail helping me drill into her flashed through my mind. One leg bent in the crook of my elbow while the other climbed up my back. She was flexible as hell, but that didn't mean I should damn near rip her hair out.

I brought my lips close to her mouth but gripped the hair at the base of her head and pulled, exposing her neck. Leilani moaned. I guided her down to the bed and climbed atop her as I kissed from her chin to her chest then just above her breasts.

"I've dreamt of your titties," I said, flicking my tongue over one pebbled nipple. "I've wanted to suck and tease then for a while."

"Less talk, more action." Leilani arched her back.

I took advantage, slipping my arm beneath her to pull her closer. I bit down and tugged her nipple before soothing it. *Less talk. Got it.* She sucked air through her teeth, whimpering and rolling her body against me. I released her hair and teased her other nipple between my thumb and forefinger.

When I feathered nips and licks from one areola to the other, she mewled and placed one hand on the back of my head—each breath she took lifting her breast further into my mouth. I slipped my arm from behind her to between her legs, pressing my thumb to her clit and feeling her shake against me.

Leilani was already soaking and I couldn't wait to taste her again. To hear the lewd sounds that had kept me company for so long. To feel every inch of her body reacting for me. I craved this woman and, like a man on his last meal, I'd take my time devouring every piece of her.

CHAPTER TWELVE

LEILANI

WHEN ALEXANDER'S fingers dipped inside me. It was over. I needed his head between my legs. I hadn't forgotten how talented his tongue had been before. Something told me he'd only gotten better.

Whatever way I felt about making these ground rules would have to wait. I needed this and so did he. Maybe we'd be able to properly focus once this was said and done. There were no weird situations and unknowns this time around.

I wasn't vulnerable and dealing with grief. Alexander wasn't potentially in a relationship or dancing between girlfriends. It was us. Just us. I moved my hand from the back of his head to the top and pushed him down my body. He chuckled.

"Let me take my time," Alexander said as he kissed just above my pussy.

"No, no," I said. "Take your time next time. Put that tongue to work so you can get that dick inside me."

His lips spread mine as he licked and sucked my clit with a loud, wet kiss. The combination of his digits moving inside me and his mouth assaulting every sensitized nerve ending was going to be the way I died. I would happily go in bliss. Everyone would know, but if I were dead it wouldn't matter.

This man had not forgotten anything. He'd remembered how to hold me—touching the spots that drove me wild, winding me up in a way only he had ever been able to do. My hands splayed at my sides the longer Alexander's fingers worked inside me.

When he added another digit, my back bowed so much the only thing left on the bed was the top of my head. I gasped and grasped at anything to keep me glued to this moment—to this sensation.

My stomach tightened and I felt my release building up. I couldn't get a sound to leave my throat. He spread my legs wider, his tongue flittering against my clit. My breaths were short. Every inch of my being focused on what Alexander was doing between my thighs.

When he slid his fingers from within me and replaced them with his tongue, the warmth was too much. I came all at once. He suckled and held me in place until he'd had his fill.

My back violently crashed down to the mattress. My hands found their way into my still wet hair. When he didn't stop licking, I felt my muscles tightening again. My legs started shaking.

"Oh, God," I managed. "Oh. Stop. No, don't. Fuck."

I tried to push him away, the feeling overwhelming me, but he clamped his arm over my waist. A hum I thought might have been Alexander saying no vibrated against my clit as his mouth moved side to side. Too much. Too sensitive. I came again. My body flushed with desire. Hot and overworked. I wanted more, but not his tongue. I needed him inside me.

"Fuck..." I struggled to form a coherent sentence. "Me." I

managed to lull my head to the side enough to see a smirk on his lips and a glisten on his chin. "Now."

"Yes, ma'am."

He rose to his feet. I used the moment to take him in. The firm muscles I'd been imagining for longer than I cared to admit. The way Alexander's veins pressed against the skin of his arms. The way he still glistened in spots from the shower we'd taken. The curve and girth of the dick I'd been able to please. I hadn't sucked him off before, but damn if I hadn't considered it more than once since that night all those years ago.

I almost wanted to hate myself for the way my thoughts had shifted yet again, but I couldn't blame them on emotions this time. I wanted him and he wanted me too. Pure carnality. As long as this stayed between us, it didn't matter. We could get over this lust and his crush would be cured. He'd see it was a sexual thing. He'd wanted something for so long and finally gotten it. He'd get over it.

As he rolled the condom down his length, I thought about all the things we could do. Alexander had been in charge last time. I'd been too in my emotions to lead anything. This time, I wanted him to see I could do more than lay there and be flipped around.

It would feel less intimate and give him a deeper angle if I was on top of him instead. As I regained the memory of how to move my limbs, he started to crawl over me. I put my hand to his chest and pushed him to the side. Alexander angled himself away, distress etched across his face.

I smiled to reassure him.

"Let me have some fun," I said. "Lay down."

He obeyed, a grin on his face. On shaky limbs, I tossed a leg over his torso and settle just above his dick. My hands roamed his chest, his rested on my thighs. He started to raise his head toward me, but I held him down with a palm pressed just beside his heart. I lifted just enough and reached behind me to angle him at my entrance.

When I slid down on Alexander, my mouth popped open. I'd forgotten how much he filled me. It was one thing to take him in my mouth. He'd been bigger than I could handle without the help of my hand, but the way he stretched my pussy was something even more.

I watched his face as his eyes melted shut and his lip tucked between his teeth. The way his fingers dug into my thighs told me this was a lot for him too. Once he was buried to the hilt, I rotated my hips, feeling the way he moved inside me with each tiny roll of my body.

"Shit, sweetheart," Alexander groaned.

I bit back a smile and threw my head toward the ceiling. After he heard Christopher call me baby girl, he immediately shifted his pet name to sweetheart. If only he knew Christopher picked it up from my mom and that was the real reason I didn't want Alexander to say it. Throwing those thoughts from my mind, I focused on him, on this connection, on these sensations.

I began lifting and twirling up to the tip of his dick before slamming back down. Our bodies worked together. He held and squeezed and rubbed every inch he could touch as I found a rhythm I liked and bounced on top of him.

Our moans and groans mingled together. My hands pressed hard against his chest. I watched him watching me before it became too intense. I leaned forward, my head cradled in the crook of his neck and my hand against the wall behind the bed.

As I felt my legs starting to shake, I gripped the sheets with my free hand. I didn't want this to be over. Not yet. But I couldn't keep it up much longer.

As if Alexander knew I was losing momentum or that I was close, his hands snaked their way up my back. He held me to him then shifted the power dynamic. He thrust his hips, pressing his dick into me with such force that I was rocking forward even more than I had been when I was in control.

I arched my chest into him—his grip on the small of my back and between my shoulder blades deepening. Alexander's lips went to my neck. I whimpered as my hand flew from the wall to grip the back of his head.

I was going to come again and that would be it. I would be wrung out in the best way, but I didn't want to fall over the edge without him coming with me. "Alex…" I moaned. "I'm. Close."

"Come for me, sweetheart," Alexander grunted. He flipped us until I was on my back. My thigh rested on his. He leaned over, tucking his arms beneath me to grip my shoulders from behind. "Come for me."

The whisper against my ear nearly undid me. *Not yet. Not yet.* My hand roamed his back. "Come with me," I said.

That must've been his breaking point. He paused and looked at me, holding eye contact as he picked up his pace again and pushed me off the cliff. Seconds later he crashed over right behind me. Alexander kissed my jawline down to the curve of my neck and slowly slid out of me.

When he climbed from the bed a few minutes later, I knew I was in trouble. I'd have to remember this was just sex. It was just sex, but as he crawled into the bed and pulled the sheet up around us, I knew he thought it was more. And maybe…

THE NEXT MORNING, I woke to the sound of the bathroom door next to my head. When I opened my eyes, I saw two things. The first was the steam escaping the room around the second thing, Alexander.

He was rubbing his hands across the top of his head in an effort to lay stray hairs flat. His abs were glistening like they had been last night. I groaned internally. The water droplets made their way slowly down, catching on the towel loosely hanging from his hips.

My mouth went dry. Damn, I wanted to fuck him. Again. *Don't do it. We have work to do.*

I clenched my jaw and started to look away when I caught Alexander giving me one of the sexiest smirks I had ever seen on any man. Then he walked over to his duffle bag sitting on the small desk.

"Didn't think you were awake yet," he said. "Forgot my clothes."

"Sure you did." I sat up, holding the blanket to my chest. "I need to brush my teeth, wash my face, and take another shower. Get dressed out here if you like."

I darted into the bathroom, taking the sheet with me. I leaned over the sink and took a couple of deep breaths. I could not have more impure thoughts about that man. We're supposed to be going back to the venue to get more pictures today.

We cannot stay in bed for the next six months. Get it together. When I straightened up to handle my morning routine, I saw him standing in the doorway, by way of the mirror.

"I heard you breathing raggedly," Alexander said. "The door was open. I just wanted to make sure you were okay."

His mouth-watering frame leaned against the space he occupied as if he were the most domestic person you could think of—a man waiting on his woman to finish up with what she was hogging. Which wasn't the case in the least.

"I'm fine." I lied. "Just morning breathing exercises."

He smirked knowingly. "Well, I need to brush my teeth as well. Mind sharing the sink?"

He hadn't put on a stitch of clothing. His body was very distracting. Unconsciously, I nodded and he walked up behind me, reaching around to turn the water on. Alexander's body brushed against mine and a small gasp escaped my lips. I did not dare look up to see our reflection in the mirror.

"You know, on second thought, I'll sort myself out after you finish," I said. "If you'll excuse me."

I carefully maneuvered around him as he went on brushing his teeth like it was nothing. Okay. In the light of the day, fucking him and sleeping with him might not have been a good idea. Damnit, he'd gotten two things out of me last night. This was not how things were supposed to be going.

CHAPTER THIRTEEN

ALEXANDER

MY MIND WAS STILL REELING over the fact that we'd had sex again. Not only that, but Leilani didn't disappear in the middle of the night as she had before. It wasn't like she could go anywhere anyway, but she'd stayed in my arms. That was something I hadn't expected. Something she seemed to be adamant she wouldn't do.

I awoke to her soft snores and wild hair. Her arm was draped across her face, but her parted lips peeked out from beneath it allowing me to see the tiny line of drool pooling on the pillow. For a moment, I couldn't do anything but drink her in. She was a dream—one I didn't want to wake up from. But we'd had more work to do.

While she seemed at ease for the most part—as if the acrobats we'd done the night before weren't affecting her in the same way as they had the first time—I wasn't sure where her head was. Leilani darted from the bathroom that morning, but then she'd calmed after her shower.

We had a quiet breakfast with Christopher and his family. I saw them eyeing us the entire time, but neither said a word. The only thing that was mentioned in length was spending time with her godchildren before we left in the afternoon.

We spent part of the morning at the venue again. Leilani had more questions she wanted to ask, plus she said it would be good to get photos in the daylight, so angles and imagery could come together for us and for Chance and Justice.

The place was beautiful, but seeing Leilani in her element was even more amazing. She wasn't shy or quiet there. She took charge and smiled through conversations like this was exactly what she was supposed to be doing every single day of her life.

Once we were back at the house, we stayed a couple of hours. I watched Leilani play with Christopher's youngest daughter. It was yet another side of her that I was getting to witness. This one was as heartwarming as the others.

Not only was she good at her job, which I'd known, but Leilani cared deeply about others in a way I hadn't seen. From the sweets for the shelter to the way she gave that three-year-old her undivided attention.

"I know you like her. Whatever you're thinking, amp up that plan ten notches." Christopher took a seat beside me, holding his one-year-old son. "Give her that young buck energy. She wouldn't have spent the night in a tiny studio-sized back house with you if you weren't family or if she didn't find you worthy of something more."

If only he knew what we'd gotten up to in that room. I kept my eyes trained on Leilani because I thought they'd betray me and spill all our secrets. Thankfully, Mercedes called Christopher to help with dinner. Unfortunately, he looked at me and held his son out for me to grab.

"Think you can get him to finish going to sleep?" Christopher asked.

My eyes grew. I shook my head. "Oh, come on. It's not that hard. He's half-sleep now. Just rock him and cradle his head," he said. "You want nieces and nephews. You might as well get ready early."

He carefully placed the little boy in my arms. I froze. I heard both Mercedes and Leilani laughing. When I looked up, I saw the woman I was growing to adore smiling at me.

"You'll be fine," Leilani said. "He falls asleep easy from what Chris told me."

Sure enough, he was out within five minutes. He didn't even fuss. Since it was starting to get late at that point, we bid the lovely family adieu and were on our way back to San Francisco by a little after five o'clock. Even though that had been the most time I'd spent with people who knew Leilani longer than my sister had, I got a new sense of her through them.

One, her other best friend was just as observant as Justice and Chance, but thankfully none of them noticed that we'd slept together. And two, while Leilani was shy and quiet, she was even more thoughtful and caring than I'd known.

We'd arrived back at her place around midnight. I was too exhausted to drive another fifteen minutes, so I crashed in the guest room. Missouri had gone out of town for an event one of the teams was having in conjunction with the players from Sacramento.

That meant we had the house to ourselves. I wanted to talk to Leilani about what happened, but I thought I should just let it be what it would be. She'd set her ground rules. We had months to do whatever we wanted. I had months to convince her I was worthy of the love I'd seen her give others.

When I awoke the next morning, I saw her walk past the door I'd left open. She was in a robe and smoothing her hair into a ponytail. I jumped from the bed and rushed to the door.

"Hey," I said.

Leilani turned around to look at me, pausing whatever audiobook had been playing on her phone. When her eyes met mine, she smiled and glanced away.

"You umm, want to eat breakfast?" I asked. "We can talk through a few more things. Like what we'll be working on next."

"I have to get to work early, actually," Leilani said. "We're doing yet another campaign and I'm overseeing the organization for this one."

I took a deep breath and nodded. I should've known it would take more than a trip together to get her really talking to me, regardless of what happened. "I'll see you in a couple of weeks, yeah?" she asked.

"Yup," I said. "I'll text you sometime later this week about everything."

"For sure." Leilani pecked my cheek and walked off to her room.

I gathered my stuff while she did whatever she needed, then knocked on her door. She opened it, her robe still on, but looser than a few minutes ago. I could see part of her shoulder and I wanted to kiss the edge of it. I cleared my throat instead.

"I'm heading out, want to lock the door behind me?"

Leilani waved me down the hall, the walk silent until I opened the front door.

"Alexander?"

"Call me Alex, Lani."

She ignored me. "The trip was nice, thanks for the breakfast stop. I love that place, and I definitely would've missed out on that meal if we kept going," she said. "The entire time we spent together was nice."

"Anytime," I said. "I hadn't been to that place in a while, but the stop was worth being late and losing our room."

Leilani's cheeks tinted red and she shifted her gaze

toward the ground. After a quick moment, she refocused on me.

"I wouldn't have seen Chris, Mercedes or the kids had we gone to the hotel," she said. "My rules still stand. I'll see you in two weeks unless one of us gets an itch that needs scratching. Work's going to keep me super busy until then, though. Text me if anything pops up, yeah?"

Unintentionally, my eyes roamed her disheveled appearance. To anyone outside of this room, we looked like two lovers saying goodbye the morning after Valentine's Day. Technically we had slept together and had a weekend of fun, but I knew better. When my eyes returned to her face, she was staring at me.

"Did you hear me or were you too busy eye-humping me?"

Focus. "I heard you. I'll text you if *anything* pops up. See you later."

SINCE WE DIDN'T EAT breakfast, I decided to stop by Sugar Crystal on Da Block. It was one of the best and oldest bakeries in town and I knew my boy was running the shop while his mom was out. The line was out of the door per usual, but I waited in it anyway. It gave me time to check in with my sister.

"How'd it go?" Justice's voice rang through loud and clear.

"Hello to you too," I said.

"Hi, brother," she huffed. "How was the viewing?"

"It was great," I said. "We sent you and Chance an email with tons of photos and a few questions. When you get a minute, check it out."

"Awesome," Justice said. "What about you and Leilani?

Y'all spend any alone time together? I know she was still pretty adamant about avoiding you."

Because she didn't want to see me after we had sex, Justice! I didn't say anything. I remained quiet and moved with the line as it got closer and closer to the door.

"I have handed you a golden opportunity," Justice said. "Use it."

I did. Trust me. "I'll be talking to her later this week about what we're doing next," I said. "We had a good time. Spent some of it together."

"Good, glad that much went well, but... hold on."

It sounded like she'd covered the phone and was talking to someone else. After a minute or two, I was tempted to hang up but the line hadn't moved enough. I'd reached the door, but it would still be another couple of minutes before I got inside.

"Sorry, I'm making sure everything is ready for Renee in her dressing room," Justice said. "Anyway, I'm glad the venue situation went well, but what about the two of you? Anything fun happen? How was the hotel?"

"I assume you haven't spoken to Chance," I said. "We were late and missed out on the hotel. Stayed at Leilani's friend Chris's spot. Remember him? He let us crash in his back house."

"Oh? And anything fun happen?" Justice paused for a moment. "No, the stylist and the makeup artist are coming in an hour. She'll be here in thirty, make sure we have her food in the fridge by then."

"Justice."

"Hold on."

She went off on a tangent for like five minutes. I finally reached the counter. My friend and his second, who was normally in the kitchen, were both taking orders.

"Jussie, I'm hanging up."

"Sorry, sorry. I'm here. Promise. Tell me how you and Leilani were."

"I told you already. We were fine. We ate breakfast on the way down, looked at the venue, and spent some time with Chris's family. It was great."

"Anything fun happen?"

Making sure my sigh was loud enough for her to hear, I took a moment before answering.

"You asked three times, sister. Nothing fun happened," I said. *Something fucking amazing did though.* "I'm getting breakfast at Sugar Crystal. Gotta go, I'm holding up the line. Love you, bye."

I hung up before she could say anything more. I'd hear it later, but there wasn't anything I could say. With my boy looking at me like I had a secret to share, I knew this day was only going to get longer.

"I do not have time for it," I said. "I need coffee and a shower."

"Who's the lucky girl?" Midnight asked, making my normal order. "Wait, you were talking to your sister, which means—"

"None of your business," I said. "Can you keep him in check, Lans?"

"That boy don't listen to nobody but his momma," Alanya said. "You three musketeers are all a mess anyway." She turned to Midnight. "The line is manageable now. I'm going back to get some stuff prepped for the second rush."

She walked off to the back before either of us could say another word. I looked at the swinging door before returning my eyes to Midnight. He shook his head and waved his hand through the air.

"How's Mama Wolfe doing by the way?" I asked.

"She's in and out of it," he sighed. "Doctors are hopeful, but we'll see."

He handed me my order. "Stay up, man. Let me know if you need anything."

He nodded and I quickly paid so I could rush to take a shower before heading to work. While I spent a lot of time at Club Haze, I didn't have to. I loved that place though, and it wasn't far from home.

Pushing thoughts of my time with Leilani, what my sister wanted to know and what was going on with Midnight out of my head, I made my weekly call to my club managers to find out how the weekend had gone.

"BARKLEY, can I see the order forms from the past couple of deliveries from all three locations?" I stopped at the entrance to his office.

He looked up from his computer, a crease forming deep between his brows. "Everything okay, boss?"

"Yeah, great. I wanted to check a couple of things," I said, "To see what worked well in certain vicinities so I could make sure the proper stuff gets ordered for the San Diego location."

"Isn't that my job? Did I screw up?"

I sighed and leaned against his door, crossing my arms. "Nah. You're fine. I'm just trying to stay busy. I'm a little on edge this week."

"If I may speak candidly?"

"You already know you can," I chuckled. "What I do?"

"Nothing, boss. You just seem out of sorts. You have ever since you got back from whatever you did last weekend. Bad date?"

"I'm good, just dealing with some personal life things," I said. He stared at me waiting for more. "My sister asked me to help plan her wedding while she's out of town. Complications are making it a little harder than I imagined."

"I see. Well, isn't her roommate an events coordinator or something like that?" Barkley asked. "Why don't you ask her for pointers?"

I looked toward the ground.

"She's the main complication," I admitted.

"Oh," he said knowingly. "In that case, remove the relationship and think of this as something that needs to come together properly for a client. For your sanity, work not to mess things up, yeah?"

"You right, Bark. Thanks. How was your daughter's christening by the way? I'm sorry I forgot to ask."

"No worries. Everything was wonderful. Our families got along; we even did a huge brunch afterward."

"I told you it would be alright," I patted the doorframe and went to walk off, but paused. "I do want to look at the order forms though, just to keep my hands and brain busy. Plus, I need to make sure to get through the audit paperwork before the end of the quarter; the earlier I start working on it, the sooner I can be done."

"Of course, I'll bring them over in a few. I'll get the tips and revenue forms as well."

As I sat at my desk, drowning out the noise coming from the club below, my phone rang. I answered when I saw Chance's name. "My sister okay?"

"Hi to you too, Alex. I spoke to her earlier, she was fine."

"Oh, okay. My bad. Hey, Chance. What's up?"

"I know you were trying to figure out how to rebrand your clubs," she said. "Haze is the one you wanted to add entertainment elements to, right?"

"Yeah. I want live shows, singers, dancers, all that."

"Okay, so I might be overstepping in more ways than one, but my best friend is going through some things over in New

York and I've been trying to persuade her to come back for months," Chance said. "She's an amazing dancer and she can sing her ass off. Classically trained, but she knows pretty much every dance style you can think of. If she has an incentive to come back, that might help all three of us."

"What are you asking, Chance?"

She sighed before my phone began buzzing against my ear. I pulled it back to see she was video-calling me. I switched over, my eyebrow raised and lips tight as the connection showed successful.

"For me, it'll help me get my best friend back. Her dream was to be on Broadway one day and things are going to holy high hell for her. She's talented as fuck, but I miss her dearly and the people she's surrounded by don't seem to be all that great," Chance said. "For her, I think it would allow her to start over and define her life on her terms and not what she thinks society expects. For you, I guarantee she'll bring in a revenue stream that your club would never receive without her."

Chance pushed the phone back and a disembodied hand started applying eye shadow to one lid as another set of fingers fluffed her hair.

"Okay, I need more than she's your friend though," I said. "I'll have to start changing up things in the club now and that means set shifts, promotions, and all that. What if she doesn't agree or if she's not as talented as you think she is?"

"I would never put friendship over business especially when it could harm either party. I love her with all my heart, but if she sucked, then that would be that. Just give her a call."

The hands started working on applying lipstick and other layers of makeup.

"You seem to be very busy," I said. "Just send me her number and name and I'll reach out as soon as I get a chance to check her out."

"Full disclosure, she's involved in a problem that's probably going to get her black-balled on Broadway," Chance said. "She needs this fresh start and you are looking for talent. I'll send you her info shortly. Thanks, kid."

"I'm not," her line cut me short when she ended the call. "... a kid."

CHAPTER FOURTEEN

LEILANI

IT HAD BEEN ALMOST a month since our unintentionally intimate trip to Oceanside. We'd had two quick sessions since. Once when I'd met up with him at his place ahead of a video call with Chance and Justice. The second was at my apartment while Missouri was out grabbing groceries.

That had been a pretty close call. Luckily, I'd worn a dress and was able to pull myself together quickly. Alexander had left the light on in the bathroom, so Missouri thought he'd come from there when he exited the hall a few minutes after me.

To say it was fun and exciting was accurate, but wrong. I was supposed to be working this out of my system, not making either of us crave it more. I'd tried to suppress it—to ignore it—this last week, though.

Yet, sitting here on a Tuesday evening with Missouri and her boyfriend made that thought difficult. They were such a cute couple, but it made me emotionally sick.

The way he cared and noticed the little things, like when she parted her lips a certain way it meant she was thirsty, so he brought her a glass of water as we continued to watch this damn rom-com.

I couldn't keep watching them be this cute. For reasons beyond me, it made me want Alexander here beside me. I'd been texting him off and on because we had things to discuss, but sometimes we'd just talk about work or how much we wanted football season to come around again.

Alexander thought it was cute that I knew nothing about the sport but liked to watch the players run up and down the field. If only he knew how much Missouri had tried to explain multiple sports to me and it had never stuck.

"I'm on the road tomorrow. I should probably be back by Thursday before heading out again on Friday. The team is getting some spring training in, but they are heading down to Anaheim," Missouri said. "I also got contracted to shoot a few players from the football team since Frisco won the Super Bowl last month. Everybody is doing something and now their quarterback is involved in some type of campaign to support adults who have lost their parents to cancer."

He must've been the athlete that was working on a book that I'd heard about around the office. I sat my phone down and glanced toward her. Missouri was supposed to come with us this weekend. That would definitely have helped keep me from falling into bed with him again.

After the video call to Chance and Justice about the venue and the update on the florist, they'd gone radio-silent. I understood they were swamped, so it took time to get back to us, but idle hands got into things.

If I was left to my own devices with Alexander again, I'd be in for another couple of rounds. I wasn't fully complaining, but I thought we'd mess around a few times throughout the six months, not three times in one. I needed a buffer.

For whatever reason, the basketball and baseball teams

Missouri photographed were extremely busy and I could've sworn one of those sports was out of season, but what did I know? I understood it was like March Madness or whatever.

Wait, was that for professionals or college? Sports weren't my forte. All that mattered was that she was barely home, and I'd be likely to have sex with Alex way more than I should. Alexander.

"Okay, Zuri. Well, keep me up to date," I said. "Oh, by the way, I want to go to a game."

She looked at me like my head had exploded in front of her. Tristan, on the other hand, laughed. Hard.

"Screw you guys," I said. "I've learned the basics."

"Yeah? What are they?" Tristan chimed in.

His little Malaysian ass nearly disappeared on the other side of Missouri because she had at least four inches on him. She was thicker than the best Bundt cake, but he was the cutest thing since sliced bread. What was most important was he knew Missouri's past and it didn't bother him nor scare him away, which made me immediately like him for that reason alone.

Missouri stopped using her given name at sixteen and her aunt started having conversations with her so they could find doctors and surgeons who were at the top of their field, and weren't judgy assholes. While she'd met Tristan a couple of years after her transition, she'd almost immediately told him. He didn't care. They'd been dating for three years now.

I couldn't be happier for her, but I honestly knew nothing about sports, even after Alexander attempted to explain football to me. Missouri had spent years doing the same thing. Except, this was basketball, which I knew a smidge about from listening to the two of them talk. Yet, she and Tristan continued to stare at me like I'd grown a second head.

They were a match made in freaking heaven—two of the

only ones who worked off Da Block because of where the stadiums and arenas were located and had a love for sports, with little interest in their biological parents. Missouri learned all about baseball and basketball during the years she'd lived with her aunt and uncle. She learned about football after graduating and became a photographer for two San Francisco teams—one of which Tristan worked for.

"I know they use a ball and then run up and down the court and they throw it in the little hoop thing," I sighed. "That's how they get points and whoever has the highest score wins. Oh... and sometimes the players get in trouble and another person or a different team gets to throw the ball from really close to try to get more points."

I said it so confidently, which only made them laugh all the harder.

"Whatever. Screw you guys. I have work to do." I hopped to my feet, shuffling from the room as they continued laughing.

Maybe I was being a brat, but I actually did need to get a few things done ahead of tomorrow. The real reason I left was that I couldn't stop thinking about Alex—Alexander— and it was starting to bother me. Instead of diving right into work, I called the one person who had no stake in where my thoughts were.

"Hey, 'sup little bit?" Christopher answered as I plopped onto the mattress.

I hated that nickname. I much rather he called me baby girl. He was the only person who I didn't get upset with when it came out of his mouth.

"Hey so, umm. I wanted your advice on something."

"Does this have anything to do with the way you and Alex were acting when y'all were here?"

"The way we were acting? What you talking about?" I rolled over on my back and stared at the ceiling.

"You wouldn't meet his eye and almost didn't acknowledge his existence during breakfast," Christopher said. "He, on the other hand, couldn't take his off you. Did y'all bang?"

"You know what? Nevermind, Christopher. I'll figure it out myself."

"Wait, chill. Hold on a second." His line went silent. I assumed he was handling something at home. I'd called like it wasn't the middle of the evening. "Okay, sorry. Cedes is on bedtime duty. Anyway, answer the question."

"No."

"No, you won't answer or no y'all didn't bang?"

I sighed. "The former."

"Okay. So, what's up?"

He'd always been like this. Never questioned things, whether Christopher believed me or not. He just moved on to the next topic. Eventually what I had to say came out and I couldn't begin to tell you how he did it, but it always happened.

"Nothing, it's alright. If I can't figure it out. I'll give you a callback."

"Okay, baby girl. Talk to you soon."

I rolled my eyes. Of course, he was like a freaking fortune teller and would indeed probably hear from me shortly. We hung up and I got to work planning out another social media campaign.

I needed to get in touch with a few of the people on my team, but I was really not in the mood. I was having a serious case of the Mondays, and the Alexanders. If I could get him off my mind, then I could create a plan and work it out before speaking to the rest of the team to flesh it out tomorrow.

By Thursday, Missouri hadn't returned from her work trip, so I was still home alone. I'd been avoiding Alexander. Beyond a few texts, because Justice and Chance had reached out, I wouldn't talk to him on the phone nor would I let him come over. The swirl of desire for him hadn't subsided, nor had the want for him to fuck me into next Sunday.

One way I'd minimized our time together was by creating a spreadsheet. The sex was good, but too much and feelings would undoubtedly get involved. A spreadsheet for the work we had to do was a way to keep our brains on track.

Alexander had been working on taking me out on this non-date night since we came back from Christopher's house, but I continued to push it off. Alexander told me if I didn't go by the end of the month, I'd have three dates with him in April since he'd missed out on February and March. That was not about to happen.

I finally agreed and said February had been taken care of when we went to breakfast. So, this weekend was non-date number two. We were supposed to go out to some ritzy spot in Nob Hill, though.

I mean he'd been nice and even productive since we started to work together, but we'd also had sex. Really good sex. I didn't want him to think this was more than just that. But, since it was a swanky place, I had to get dressed up. I'd just have to remind him what this time together was all about.

I'd focus on wedding planning. We had to get on top of the dresses and suits now. I'd narrowed down the shops to two locations for the bridesmaids' dresses. Since each bride had a custom gown being made and the designer worked out of one of the two locations, we'd use both boutiques to find the outfits for the rest of the bridal party.

I couldn't see them walking down the aisle in anything less than what one of Chance's friends designed for each of them and had started not long after we found out about the wedding.

This, by far, was one of the most important steps. We were going to go check on the progress of the gowns and try to find something that would look great on multiple different-shaped women. With the venue already selected, and the florist pretty much taken care of, things were coming together well.

We could've gotten a couple of other situations handled over the past month if we weren't fucking every time we were in each other's presence, but it was fine. I was beginning to feel like a pro at this wedding planning stuff. I knew it would all work out in the end.

Through texts and the spreadsheet, Alexander gave input and helped book the cake design session for this weekend as well. Since we'd be seeing each other whether I wanted to or not, I decided to add some more time in for bachelorette party planning too.

I didn't know about him, but I thought ahead, with the right part of my body. To make sure I wouldn't be needed at the office tomorrow, I brought all the important information for my work project home and assigned other pieces to the rest of my team. I could work on wedding stuff and prep the event with the publisher at the same time that way.

CHAPTER FIFTEEN

LEILANI

"I CANNOT GET you off my mind. What the hell kind of hoodoo did you put on me?"

Alexander quirked an eyebrow, the ghost of a grin on his lips. I'd opened the front door to let him in. He stood there in a sleek, black dress shirt with the top two buttons undone. He had on white pants and suspenders, which threw me for a moment, but he looked good enough to eat. Swallowing the building saliva, I couldn't help but stare.

He surveyed my body like it was a new treasure he discovered. When his eyes met mine, he bit his lip, lifting out of the position he'd been leaned into. When he came inside the apartment and pushed the door closed behind him, I was forced to take a few steps back.

Did I say that aloud? I had to change the subject quickly. "I was gonna get dressed up but changed my mind. I'm almost ready. Give me five minutes."

The grin that had been playing on his lips blossomed into a full smile, teeth and all. Alexander raised a bottle of champagne I hadn't noticed he was holding. "Thought we could stay in instead of going out. I could make you a meal."

"Umm, okay. Sure."

Since I'd been dressed in a t-shirt, oversized cardigan, and jeans, I was fine with that. His attire wasn't exactly equal to mine, and I damn sure wasn't in the mood to change. Unconsciously, I backed toward the couch. When I ran into it, I fell into a seat. He chuckled and he walked over to the kitchen, returning with two champagne flutes moments later.

"Aren't you going to make me a meal?"

"I'm about to do that right now. Just one question first."

Squinting suspiciously at Alexander, I kept my eyes trained on his movements as he sat down beside me. He was extremely close, so much so that I had to put a few inches between us.

"What?" I asked.

"On the couch or in the bed?" His attention never dropped my eyes.

My head pulled away and shook in shock for what felt like much too long. That sly, sexy smile of his crept across his face. "You better be talking about food, boy."

"Not a boy, Lani." Alexander bit the side of his lip and leaned back slightly. "But yeah, something like that. So… your room or here on the couch?"

"I'm not trying to crumb up my bed." I worked to stay focused. Maybe he was just teasing and I was the one who couldn't keep my head on straight. "I mean, we can have it here, but why not at the table?"

Alexander's smile grew wider as he stood up, putting out a hand for me. "And so it has been proclaimed."

Both flutes remained in hand, but he must've left the champagne in the kitchen knowing I would suggest eating in there. I stood without the help of his hand and walked into the kitchen.

"So, what are you going to make me?" I said taking a seat at the table.

"Satisfied."

Satisfied? I shivered. I wasn't here for this tomfoolery. We were supposed to be eating, not messing around. I was focused on having a normal regular conversation with him, but damn if he wasn't seriously tempting me. "Chile, you got about two seconds to quit pla—"

Alexander knelt in front of me and placed his hands on my thighs before I could finish my threat. The flutes were sitting on the table beside the champagne. I wasn't sure when he became a ninja, but I had to lean back in my chair when I saw how close he'd gotten. *Fuck me.*

"That's two, sweetheart. You know, in baseball at three strikes you're out, right? Well, my rules are a little different, and you'll soon find out if you try me one more time," Alexander caressed up the inseam of my pants. "You seem to somehow still have it stuck in your head that I'm a youngin'. I'm not, and you should know that. But I'm always game for a gamble."

My heart pounded in my chest. His warm hands on my thighs, the heat seeping through the fabric.

"I'm betting in the next sixty seconds you'll be so curious that you'll make that third strike happen just to find out what I'll do. Just how much I'll satisfy you yet again," Alexander said. "You like it. Admit it, or you could just step up to the plate and let me lick it clean."

Refusing to let him know he was affecting me more than I was willing to admit, I stood up, forcing him to fall back. I grabbed the champagne from the table, stepped around him, and went toward the sink to pop the cork—which took a couple of tries.

After, I grabbed the closest cup and poured myself a glass. A hearty swallow later, I turned to see him standing where

I'd left him. I rested myself against the counter, took a sip, and steeled my nerves.

"Alright, *kid*. That was more than sixty seconds, guess you lost that little bet. Now again, where's my meal?"

Alexander stalked over, trapping me between his arms. With him inches from my face, I had to lean back to create some distance. It made our bodies from our chests down touch. In some cruel twist of fate, our heartbeats had already aligned.

"Want to back up?" I asked.

"Do you want me to?"

Honestly, I didn't, but we had to take a break at some point. This was why I shouldn't have made those damn ground rules. I put myself in this situation. I told Alexander we could have it whenever we wanted, and, fuck if he wasn't making it abundantly clear he wanted it right now.

The annoying part was that he knew I wanted it to. No matter what came out of my mouth, my body was betraying me, giving him whatever signals he needed. This was why I'd switched to those damn spreadsheets. I had a decision to make. My head responded with a hard no. His gaze dropped to my lips.

"May I kiss you?"

"We agreed to no kissing on the lips," I said. "How about that meal instead?"

"Right, well I hoped to make you my main course. We could talk after that. Order in and go from there?"

My stomach dropped. Alexander slowly took my glass from me, sitting it on the far end of the counter before lifting me onto it. I couldn't stop my body from leaning toward him.

Fuck I kissed him. Fuck, a kiss? What the fuck just happened? No. No. No. The sensation of our mouths moving together dropped straight between my thighs.

I wanted this man more than I thought. Like, I wanted Alexander. My hands found the back of his neck, pulling him closer to deepen the embrace. He dipped under the hem of my shirt at the small of my back and ripped it up the middle.

"Alexander." I gasped, pulling back to find him all smiles.

"Whoops. Gonna have to buy you another one."

I narrowed my eyes at him as I felt air hit my back. He gripped his shirt at the opening and buttons went flying in multiple directions as he yanked it apart.

"Now, we're even," he said.

I wasn't sure how I missed the tribal tattoo and Greek insignia around his bicep all those times before, but it was very much distracting now. I wanted to trace my tongue over it, but instead, I used my fingers.

I'd ask him about it later, right now, I wanted to get back to what I said I wouldn't do. I pulled Alexander flush against me, our lips meeting once more. He urged my mouth open with the swipe of his tongue.

Complying with his request, I drove mine into his first. He'd always seen me as the shy, quiet, reserved ball of fire ready to ignite, but he'd learned over the past month I was much more than that. I'd kept giving him little pieces of me. I didn't want the feelings, but they were creeping in. I'd worry about that at another time. Right now, I needed the sensation of him inside me.

After a few minutes of hands and mouths traveling and fumbling across our bodies, his suspenders hung from his hips with his belt laying like an unimportant memory halfway under the counter on the opposite side of the kitchen. I hopped down to come out of my jeans. He took the opportunity to spin us around and back me over the table, lying me flat.

By the time I'd sat up on my elbows, my pants had joined the scatter of clothing around the room. I was left in my bra and panties. His slacks and dress shoes had him looking ever the 90s R&B singer. When he dropped to his knees, I readjusted so I could watch him as he kissed from ankle up my leg, reaching the crease of my thigh and nibbling ever so lightly. That elicited a whimper I hadn't intended to make.

He pushed my foot up to the table so my leg rested in a bent position. Angling my body to the side, I saw and felt him repeat the same agonizing process on the other side. When he planted my other heel, he took the time to spread them out to the far edges, and every muscle between my legs tightened under his observation. He wanted to pull a reaction out of me and knew exactly how to do it.

"Lani, may I have that meal now?" Alexander's index and middle fingers hooked into my panties at my hips.

The moment I said yes, I knew he'd shred them. But at this point, I didn't care. I needed the satisfaction he promised. Nodding, the tearing sounded and the lace fabric loosened before falling away. Even if I wanted to get angry, his lips found mine wet and needy within seconds.

His warm, wide tongue lapped up what had already leaked from me. My head fell back, mouth agape as I realized I wanted—craved—this more than I thought. Whimpers and shuddering breaths fell from my lips as a knock sounded at the door.

Alexander didn't even pretend to stop, just kept going, faster, deeper, more longingly, making me damn near lose my mind. My muscles started tightening. *Already?* Then another knock. I gasped and gripped the edges of the table above my head, trying to prolong the feeling, but I knew I was close, the tightening of muscles and sensations building.

The third knock couldn't break my zeroed-in focus until… "Lani?"

My eyes fluttered open and I glanced over to see my

bedroom door ajar, Alexander's concerned head peeking inside. *A dream? A freaking sex dream... about Alex—Alexander?*

Looking around slowly, my head and heart were pounding, one from the dream, but the other I wasn't sure about. A sheen of sweat coated every inch of me, especially what was covered by the blanket. The scratchiness of my throat made it hard to even swallow my saliva.

"You okay? You look like crap." Alexander didn't come in, but he pushed the door the rest of the way, scanning the room.

"My head hurts." I croaked. With my curtains drawn, I couldn't guesstimate the hour. "What time is it?"

"After ten, I tried texting and calling, but you didn't answer. Eventually, I got ahold of Missouri and she said she hadn't been home in a couple of days so I came to check on you," Alexander said. "When you didn't answer the door, I used the spare key Justice gave me to make sure everything was okay."

My skin felt like it was on fire and I'd been stuffed inside an oven. My heartbeat made my head vibrate with an intensity that had no end. Even with my eyes shut, the small bit of light felt like it was being burned into my retinas. The bed dipped on my left, then I felt a cool pressure on my forehead.

"Damn, you're burning up. I'll be right back."

Before I could protest, Alexander left the room.

CHAPTER SIXTEEN

ALEXANDER

THE LAST THING I expected when I came over was to find Leilani in this condition. I was prepared to ask why she was ignoring me today, and had been keeping me at a distance for weeks, but I found her sickly. I hated to see her like this. I went over to the bathroom, searching for a thermometer and checking if they had medication for fever, flu, or cold.

After I got a better sense of her symptoms, I could give her the right stuff. Grabbing what I needed from the cabinet, I went back to her room and told her to leave the thermometer under her tongue. On a quick trip to the kitchen, I checked to see what they had that I could use to make her food. I found crackers, bread, items for soup and tea.

Taking care of her, even this little bit, gave me a sense of importance. My heart ached because Leilani looked like she was an extreme discomfort, but knowing I might be able to help sent butterflies into my gut.

"What's your temperature, sweetheart?"

She groaned but feebly lifted the thermometer to me. 99.8°. Great. She had a fever, which meant it was likely she had the flu. I didn't care though because even if I took her to the hospital, I wouldn't be leaving her side.

After running down how she felt, it was confirmed. I knew I needed to get more fluids to keep her well hydrated. She also needed to shower because she was sweating profusely under the blankets.

"I don't want to," Leilani whined. "Can't I just lay here?"

The way I knew she wasn't feeling good started when she didn't berate me for barging into her room. "Shower, Leilani. Come on, I'm not going to stand in there and keep watch unless you start acting up or I hear a loud thud."

"You can't." She paused to cough into her pillow. "You can't come in the bathroom with me."

"I won't," I said. *Not this time.* "Only going to help you to the door."

After what became a battle with an infant, she was in the tub instead of the shower. Leilani said she was light-headed and wanted to sit. It allowed me the time to strip her bed to wash her sheets. I carefully looked through her linens, finding another set to redress her mattress. After that, I went about starting the soup.

Every ten minutes, I checked on her and she responded, "same as I was last time you asked," which let me know she wasn't as near death as she appeared. Damn that smart-ass mouth of hers. If she wasn't feeling bad, I'd get her to put it to work. After nearly an hour passed and I helped her back to her room, she stared at the bed for a long moment.

"You sweated through your sheets, I thought it nice to have fresh ones. Sorry if I overstepped."

"No, it's fine, just didn't think you knew where all my stuff was." Leilani climbed into bed with my assistance. "You creeping in my crap when I'm not home?"

"Not anymore," I said.

She attempted to squint her eyes at me, but it turned into more of a grimace.

"Kidding, but I quickly looked through your things and found these," I said. "I put them on and stuff the other set in the washer, well the dryer now."

"Thank you." Leilani laid down, closed her eyes and pulled the blanket up to her chin.

"You need to eat and drink something. When's the last time you did either?"

"Before bed yesterday."

I left, returning with a cup of tea and a tumbler of water. "Your soup is almost done. You want some crackers or something for now?"

"Only sleep, please."

I shook my head. "After you drink some of this tea, at least."

She sighed and struggled to get up before sipping the tea a few times. I didn't say anything, but the position she was in looked uncomfortable as hell. Long as she drank something I would be happy.

She set the mug down to lift herself out of the awkward angle she'd been in. I helped her, putting a pillow behind her back and pushing her hair out of her face.

"Ugh, I know I look like shit. Just leave me to die in embarrassment, please."

I didn't respond. Instead, I handed Leilani the mug and she pouted before taking another sip. It took her twenty minutes or so to drink the entire thing. When she finished, she looked at me sleepily. "I'll eat when I wake up. Sleep now, okay?"

"Alright."

"You don't need to stay after the food is done," she mumbled. "I don't want to steal your Friday away."

"The only thing I'd been focused on beyond this wedding

stuff was the progress of the San Diego location. It's going well," I said. "I don't have to be at the club unless I want to, so I let everyone know I would be gone over the weekend and to contact me if something was really bad."

"Wonderful." Leilani didn't sound happy. "I don't want you getting sick because of me. Leave me some medicine on my table and I'll be fine."

"I'm not going anywhere unless Missouri comes back or you need to go to the doctor, Leilani. I'm here. You need to be taken care of, so let me do that."

"But if you catch the flu—"

"If I do, I do. I'll be fine. Get some rest, I'm going to get you some meds and more fluids."

"Thank you," Leilani muttered, already half-asleep.

Because it was obvious we weren't going to make it to any of our appointments this weekend, I called to reschedule them. I also shot a text to my sister, Chance and Missouri letting them know that Leilani caught the flu and we were staying in.

Almost immediately I got a message from Missouri telling me to keep her updated and that she would get home as soon as she could. I ordered medicine, juice, and a few other things through one of the apps on my phone and met the delivery person on the ground floor so they wouldn't have to lug it up to the top.

While there was an elevator, I thought it nicer and easier to meet the person, than have to wait for however long it might take them to find their way to the right apartment. The grocery store over on Divisadero Street was hard enough to navigate. And leaving the area was hell because of all the boutiques, restaurants and my club. Once I had everything I needed, I set about making sure Leilani was okay.

Every few hours, I took her temperature, and only once

did it threaten to top 103°. When it hit 101.2°, I was ready to take her to her doctor, but she refused to go. Keeping a close eye on her throughout the day probably would've driven her batty, if she hadn't slept three-quarters of the time, but I wanted to make sure her symptoms didn't get worse.

It had taken her a while, but she ate an entire bowl of soup and managed to only throw up on me once. She apologized near tears, but it didn't bother me. I could wash my clothes and take a shower and everything would be okay.

Luckily, I kept a few outfits here for whenever I spent the night and needed to clean up because I was short on time. Otherwise, I'd have been walking around in a towel. That probably wouldn't have gone over well.

In this case, I doubt Leilani would've acted on anything, but the temptation already felt palpable, even in her current state. Whenever she was awake, she kept her eyes on me. She wore very little because she was so hot from the fever, but stayed bundled in the covers because she was also cold.

After she went to sleep again, I got my all-togethers, all together, making sure I ate and drank fluids as well as took some medicine because a headache had set in. After folding her sheets and blankets, I washed my vomit-filled clothes then did her laundry, too.

Instead of sleeping in the extra room, I slept on a cot beside her bed so I could check her temperature throughout the night and help her when she needed to go to the bathroom from all the liquid she was drinking. I didn't expect her to be as dizzy as she'd been, but I was glad I could be there.

"Hey, everything alright?" I spoke low as I snuck out of her room when Justice called.

"Why are you whispering?"

"Leilani is sleep, didn't want to wake her."

"Sleep? It's pretty early over there. What happened?"

Realizing she must've missed the texts I sent her, I went about running down what had been going on.

"You're so sweet, you didn't have to do that."

"With Zuri off on business, and you gone as well, I needed to make sure she didn't pass out or something while she was alone."

"Are you cooking and cleaning and waiting on her hand and foot?"

"She's been in bed much of the time." I rolled my eyes. "I made her soup like my mom did for us when we were feverish. I think she'll be fine, I got things handled here."

"How cute," Justice crooned. "Thanks for watching over her. Did you tell her dad?"

"Umm, no. I didn't call her father to say she was sick and I was taking care of her. That seems excessive."

"She's close to him is all. I'll let him know. I was calling to ask why we hadn't heard about cake stuff, but I see why," Justice said. "Keep me posted on her, talk to you later brother."

"Love you, sister. I'll shoot you a text when she starts feeling better."

"Love you too. I'll pay better attention to my messages."

By Saturday night, Leilani had told me to sleep in bed with her because she didn't want me hurting my back lying on the ground. First, she tried to persuade me to go to the guest room, but I said I wouldn't leave her side so I could make sure she had whatever she needed.

After trying to get me to go, she gave up and tossed her arm behind her toward the empty space that was there. Leilani had been able to take a shower, even though there were two because she threw up again, this time all over herself and her side of the bed—another laundry trip. Embarrassment kept her quiet a lot, but she let me help her and didn't complain about anything I did.

At one point, I woke to find Leilani snuggled into my side. I wanted to pull her closer because this had to be a dream, but I knew if I reacted, she'd likely move away. The feel of her body close to mine was enough to have me falling back into an easy sleep.

I wanted this regularly. I wanted Leilani to know this was something we could be. Not because she was sick, but because she deserved this attention. This love. This feeling. This comfort.

My eyes flew open in the darkened room. *Love?* Shit, as long as I'd pined after Leilani, I never thought it to be that until now. Did I love her? I mean, we'd had sex a few times, but that wasn't love. Me being here when she needed someone, that was love.

Watching her play with her Goddaughter and feeling a warmth in my chest, that was love. Building that damn spreadsheet with her even though I knew she was using that as a way to keep us apart because we kept fucking, that was love. *Oh god.*

I was in love with Leilani. In four months, she'd be walking away from me because this was just sex for her. I had to figure out how to tell her we'd passed that stage. This was much more than that now.

Sunday morning, she sat up on her own and was halfway out of the bed, when I had to catch her to keep her from tipping over. I was still partially asleep given the fact that I spent much of the night dreaming of her.

"I think I can make it on my own, Alexander. Let me try."

"Sure. I'll walk behind you, just in case though."

Leilani indeed made it to the bathroom by herself, an improvement for sure. I went to make both of us a mug of tea. When I returned to the room, I found her sitting halfway up like she was waiting on me.

"Crackers and soup or—"

"I know how I got sick," she said. "I'm going to punch that person when I see them tomorrow."

"I doubt you feel good enough to go in, but answer the question you didn't let me finish."

"Crackers only please." Leilani sniffled and readjusted as I headed her the green tea. "The PR manager was coughing and sneezing all over the place on Wednesday and Thursday; the bastard had to have gotten me sick. I'm going off when I see him."

"Bring up hygiene and OSHA, I'm pretty sure knowing you're ill and bringing it to your workplace is a violation of rights for others. If you hadn't taken some time off, you'd be in a spot."

"Yeah, I'll look into it."

Both of us slept the rest of the day away. I didn't say it, but Leilani had probably gotten me a little sick because I refused not to be around her. I didn't feel as bad as she did, but I knew I'd need to sanitize the house as best I could before Missouri got back. The last thing I wanted was for somebody else to get sick because of us.

On Monday morning, I answered a few emails and made sure to try to keep track of texts and phone calls, but I was tired and would rather lay with Leilani than think about anything else.

Early in the afternoon, I couldn't help myself. My lips pressed softly against her forehead, and then I slipped away to make another grocery order. I couldn't remember all that was in the kitchen, so I went to peek through the cabinets and the fridge again.

I ordered the cleaning supplies as well, then waited for everything to arrive. I made a light dinner, and then put the food away. After wiping down everywhere I'd been, I went back to her room.

We ate in her bed, me at the foot and her at the head,

before I told her everything I'd taken care of. After chatting for a few hours, we both were tired. She'd slept in my arms again, but this time when I awoke, she hadn't moved. I checked my phone to see the time and found a text from Missouri.

Leilani let me know she'd be back in the morning. Since I wasn't sure if I was sick or contagious, I decided to leave before then. After turning on the bedside lamp, I rubbed her shoulder until she woke up. She groggily turned over to look at me.

"Missouri will be here in a couple of hours," I said. "I'm going to take off because I don't want to get her sick if I am."

Leilani nodded and shifted her body slowly until she was facing me.

"Thank you for taking care of me, and getting yourself sick because we both know you are," she smiled. "Please take care of yourself. I feel a lot better, even though my head is still kicking my ass."

"I'm not sick, but anytime," I said. "I told you I'm not the brat I used to be. I'm going to take a quick shower and head out."

"Don't shower then go out in the cold," she scolded me. "If you're going to clean up, then just stay here with me."

"Gotta make sure I don't get Missouri sick if I caught your flu," I said. "I'll just get my stuff together and take one when I get home then."

Leilani smiled and closed her eyes. "Let me know when you make it home."

I resisted the urge to kiss her lips. Instead, I dropped one on her cheek. After I gathered my stuff, I started to walk out of her room but paused to look at her a beat longer. Leilani was watching me.

"You know you my girl, right?" I asked. "I know I tormented you for years, and it was all fun and games then but I'm not a kid anymore. Even with what has been happening between us, no matter what, you my girl. I'd never leave you high or dry. While I might want more even if you don't, I'll always be here for you. I'm glad you're feeling better, and I could help you out."

Leilani's eyes glazed over for a moment before she refocused and a smile graced her face. The sound of her agreement filtered over me. I smiled before walking off down the hall.

"See you in the morning. Eat more soup if you get hungry."

"Hey, wait." Her voice and a cough carried down the hall. "How'd you get in the apartment in the first place?"

I had my hand on the knob. Her comment made me chuckle. It took her long enough to bring that up again.

"Don't you think it's a little late to ask that?" I called. "Never mind. Spare key. Remember I said I used the one Justice gave me? She did that years ago. Bye."

When I made it to my car, I got a call from Barkley who needed me to come in and handle something with a discrepancy a vendor refused to adjust unless he spoke to the owner. I hadn't made my weekly check-in call, so I must've missed something. Even though it was the middle of the night, I didn't want this to carry over past the morning if it didn't have to.

Apparently, the club and bar managers weren't high enough for the prick, and they'd tried through much of the day. I could feel my symptoms getting worse, but I knew if I didn't take care of it, things would get out of hand. The best I could do was not touch anyone or anything and get in and out as quickly as possible. My bed and shower would have to wait a while longer.

CHAPTER SEVENTEEN

LEILANI

I HEARD the front door close. I was left lying in the middle of my bed slightly aroused, partially confused and completely at a loss for words. Between the dream I had before Alexander arrived and how attentive he'd been over the past few days; I knew I'd actually started to develop real feelings.

His spiel about always being here even if I didn't want more pulled at my heartstrings. I didn't know what the hell to make of what was going through my mind right now. Him taking care of me was unexpected, but not surprising.

I remembered moments in the distant past where he'd been sweet and helpful to both me and Justice. When he'd visited our apartment in the early days, Alexander had times of being kind then too. It wasn't always bad. Now, even when I needed help getting dressed after one of my showers, he didn't try anything nor did he make comments.

I felt bad about getting him sick. The moment he started taking medicine with me, I knew. He'd looked as exhausted as I felt, but he didn't complain. How I'd ever face him after throwing up all over his lap, myself, and the floor, I didn't know, but I'd have to.

As crappy as I felt, I'd never let a man take care of me besides my father. But something about Alexander's attentiveness and lack of regard for falling ill himself made me smile, even if only internally. I wished I could at least make sure he was alright, but two sick people couldn't do much for each other.

When I'd felt good enough and he told me he'd taken care of rebooking everything I'd tried to pack into the weekend, I couldn't help but see him in a different light. He wasn't as big-headed and childish as I'd made him out to be.

I mean, he did own three successful nightclubs and had a fourth coming soon. Something about his business ethic and ability to get things done had to contribute to that. We'd talked about him wanting to expand each location and make it into something even bigger and better.

After seeing how Alexander managed to work in crisis, me being one of the two issues he'd dealt with in the past several weeks, I figured he probably did good in his business life as well. The last thing I wanted was to fully see him as the grown man I knew he was deep down.

Regardless of how much I tried avoiding it, it started filtering its way into my dreams. I'd thought about him every time my eyes closed this weekend, from taking care of me physically, to mentally and emotionally being there. I didn't know what to make of my thoughts. This was scary as hell to me.

I decided to text the one individual who didn't have some type of personal stake in the situation, once again. Like I already knew when he'd said it a little while ago, he'd be hearing from me. With it close to midnight, I figured he'd respond in the morning before he took the kids to school and went into the office.

Of course, I was incorrect, confirmed by my phone ringing not five minutes later.

"Lani, honey what's wrong?" It wasn't Christopher, it was Mercedes. She damn sure should have been asleep. She taught mommy and me yoga at six in the morning.

"Cedes, I'm sorry, I know it's late. I didn't need anything tonight. Working through things in my brain right now. Thought Chris might be able to help. My bad if I woke either of you."

"He's the one who told me to call. He's pretty sure this has something to do with Alex."

I sighed and got out of bed, moving slowly down the hall to the sectional that took up most of the living room. "Why would he think that?"

"Well, when y'all arrived everything was fine. Both of y'all were kind of annoyed but overall, like relaxed and comfortable. Kind of how it used to be those few times Alexander had tagged along with you, Missouri and Justice to hang out with us. Pretty sure that was when he'd just started college," Mercedes said. "I remember him at the wedding, eyes glued to you. Then after that, when Justice or Chris invited him places, how much you wanted to choke him, it was laughable."

I growled, but she kept at it.

"Y'all were always at each other's throats and it was pretty much the only time you weren't calm and collected. Anyway, I'll stop the trip down memory lane. That Saturday after y'all got back from the venue, y'all were different. You barely looked at him, hardly acknowledged him, but he stared at you like you were a sun goddess gracing him with your presence. Then on Sunday, both of you like ignored each other. It was weird. I thought y'all got it in and then regretted it, or you told him he was trash, or he gave you some bomb head, but you wouldn't let him go any further. I mean my mind was heading toward the gutter. I drug Chris down into it too. Now I've got to know. So, tell mama what's going on."

Observant didn't begin to describe this woman. As an instructor, Mercedes did need to pick up on things to make sure she and her students were practicing safely. It didn't mean she needed to have an imagination like she did. Fighting back a laugh because it would only make me cough, I shook my head.

"Well, well, okay, umm. He annoyed me per usual, but…"

"Go on, don't pause now. Let it pour out. I want to hear the rest of this excuse."

A person might think she was a therapist or counselor. Not the nicest, but definitely the most straightforward—especially with how she got people to talk, like really talk. I shouldn't tell her about what happened in the past or what we'd agreed to while we were there, but I needed advice from someone.

"We've been having sex," I said. Mercedes' pause made me squirm a bit, forcing me to continue. "It started when we were there. Sorry. But, umm yeah. We messed around there and it's been a couple more times since. Less than an hour ago he said he wanted more, but I don't know if that's a good thing."

"Why is it not a good thing? Y'all both grown. He is not a child, and I mean he is attractive as hell." Mumbles in the background sounded like Christopher complaining. "Hush husband. Stay out of my conversation."

I attempted to fight my laugh because I didn't want to break into a coughing fit. Thankfully, the chuckle I let out didn't take me there.

"I get it. He's your friend's brother and he's, what, ten-ish years younger? It don't matter though because he's an adult. Take that boy for a test drive. Better keep getting that young dick energy while he's hounding after you. Give him one real good trip around the block. If more turns out to be bad, then pump the breaks and let the moment blow in the wind. You can go back to hating him."

"It's a seven year difference, but I don't know about that. If things go bad between us, I don't want it to cause an issue with me and my best friend. I should just focus on getting all this stuff ready for Justice." I laid on the couch after a sigh. My head had started pounding. "I hate that she dumped this in my lap. Like, I adore her, but I want to choke her. All of this is her fault. I think I like him. Like, really like him."

"Wait what?"

I shouldn't have said anything, but this was why I'd called. I might as well lay it all out there. I needed help figuring this out. "Well, he was really sweet this weekend. I'm getting over the flu. He spent the time he was here taking care of me. Slept in my bed. I woke up and was in his arms, it tripped me out. This happened twice."

"Well, ma'am."

"Mercedes, nothing happened this time. He just made sure I ate and took medicine."

"Okay, fine. Back to the other stuff you said, though. You were very specific with the age gap there, Lani," she chuckled. "Look, think about it. I think you're wound up pretty tight and need to cut loose. Have some fun, baby girl, even if it's with your best friend's younger brother. It sounds like y'all are closer than you think. Chris and I love you. Call us if anything, okay? We both definitely need to get a couple of hours of sleep."

I half-smiled before ending the call. Christopher had always known what to say, but Mercedes jumped into my head and took over. She was a good person, but man could she be a bad influence sometimes.

This seemed like odd advice, but I wouldn't think about it for now. I tried to watch a movie to distract myself, but gave up part of the way through and went back to bed. I turned on an audiobook instead. My headache subsided, but now I had to clear my mind of the boy whom I'd started finally really seeing as a grown man.

Since it was technically Tuesday, I could occupy myself with work once the sun rose, even if only a little. I'd stay home, but I hadn't checked on the progress of the project all weekend and we needed to have everything ready in a few days.

A couple of days later, I hadn't seen or heard from Alex, which was kind of weird since he'd been so attentive while he was here. I figured he was getting over his sickness himself, but I had no real time to think about it. I wanted to go by his house, but working from home and my weakened body made that a little difficult.

I texted a few times to check on him but didn't get any response. Maybe he was sleeping as much as I had. I knew he had rescheduled everything for the upcoming weekend, which was perfect because I had the time off due to our big event happening tomorrow.

Since I couldn't get ahold of him, I took to focusing on what I could. My nausea hadn't completely subsided nor had the weakness I felt, but Missouri and Tristan helped.

The small, light meals had been the best part. After Alexander left, I thought anything beyond the soup and crackers we'd been living on would make me upchuck, but I was okay. I missed the attention and care I got from him, but when I realized I'd actually thought that, the idea of wanting him around me vanished.

I was mentally exhausted from the back-and-forth battle to keep my mind off said person and the dreams that kept happening. Plus, I'd been forced to watch the lovey-dovey, happy-go-lucky relationship between Missouri and Tristan, which was not helping. The sooner I was back to one hundred percent, the better, because I could barely deal.

Thankfully, work had me swamped, and getting back on track with the wedding planning presented itself as a second job. I hated this, mostly because it forced me to look at things I'd never imagined wanting for myself. I craved a feeling I never expected to rest in the pit of my stomach.

Affection—not what I got from my friends or my dad. Something more intimate. Something long-term. Something I'd experienced last weekend. That wasn't what was bothering me, though. It wasn't what kept me up at all odd hours of the night. What did that was that I wanted that connection with Alexander.

I couldn't focus on that too much. I still hadn't chosen whether to actually ask for more with him or not. It was unnerving to think about what that truly would mean. I couldn't make sense of it all, even after talking with Mercedes. The only other person I thought might give me answers that made sense was my dad. Being around him would probably help me feel better.

Hopefully, after talking to him I could make the algorithm of what-the-hell play out any other way in my mind. He was a teacher, after all. He should definitely have the answers I sought.

CHAPTER EIGHTEEN

ALEXANDER

I FINALLY PULLED myself together and left my home after a couple of days of dragging myself from room to room around the house. I'd avoided all sources of light that weren't my fridge or the tiny lamp in my bathroom. Now, it was the middle of the afternoon on Wednesday, but I could go to the office for a change of scenery and to get work done.

Tons of emails, texts, and missed calls appeared on my phone and I knew I'd have a lot of talking to do, which only agitated my brain all the more. Leilani checked in on more than one occasion, asking if I was okay since I hadn't gotten in touch.

She also suggested we schedule any other future outings a few weeks out since she wasn't sure how long it would take either of us to be in tip-top shape again. I couldn't agree more. She sent emails and updated the spreadsheet so I could stay on track with everything.

I had messages from Barkley letting me know things with the bars were in order. The information had been left in my physical dropbox, which I'd grabbed on my way into the club.

My managers sent their emails, including the Sunday round-up since I was too sick to care when I'd gone on Monday night. Barkley must've let them know. Vendors, contractors, and talent had reached out as well. Since I'd said I wanted to rebrand Club Haze as an entertainment joint, people were putting their hats in the mix.

Beyond Leilani and work, Justice and Chance called a few times to see if I was okay. I guessed they'd talked to Leilani, or they figured I'd gotten sick since I stayed with her all weekend. After a day of me not responding they said they'd kick my ass when they got back if I didn't get in touch with them by Friday.

Vowing to get back to Leilani once I took care of some of this—so she wouldn't think I avoided her purposely—I made back-to-back business calls, starting with the one that felt the most important.

"Hello?" A sultry voice filtered through the phone.

"Hi, this is Alexander Rutherford. Am I speaking with Ego Adams?"

"Little Alex? Chance told me to expect your call. Just call me Ego."

Hadn't heard that nickname since I was a kid. When Justice first brought her then-girlfriend around, she started calling me that, and I'd hoped we'd outgrown it after all these years. Apparently, Chance had shared my nickname with her friend. Shielding my eyes from the beating light overhead, I ignored the reference.

"Glad she made you aware. From what I understand you're in a bit of a squeeze and may be looking to start up something new. Is that true?"

"I'm fine. Don't know what she told you, but I have no plans on coming home. I'm on Broadway and just making a name for myself."

I wasn't in the mood to do the back-and-forth thing. I let

Ego know I'd read the articles about her alleged affair with the producer for the show she was supposed to be in. She was silent the entire time I spoke. I also let her know Chance had been in touch with me and wanted her to come home rather than stay there.

I even told Ego why I thought her talent would be better suited for my club, but only if she wanted to be there. I'd watched a few videos of her dancing. She was great, but I didn't have time for anything wishy-washy. I did my best to keep a calm, soothing voice, but this migraine was kicking my ass. While I was finally over the fever and super sick part of the flu, I still had to get my head to stop pounding whenever it felt like it.

Her long exhale sounded on the other end of the phone before a silence. I pulled the device away from my ear, checking to see if she'd hung up on me.

"Are you going to respond?" I asked.

"I can't run away because of this. I'll take care of it. That offer though… I don't have a group or anything."

"If you take me up on it, we can work out the details."

"I'm not interested," she said.

"Okay, sure. Well, it's a standing offer for now. Don't know how long it'll last."

"Alright. I have to go."

"Bye, Ego, and good luck with everything."

What sounded like a tired huff filtered through the phone before, "Thank you. I'll, um, I'll let you know what I decide."

After we ended the call, I refocused on the proposals and other documents in front of me. While I couldn't do anything with how I wanted to make adjustments to this club just yet, I could move forward with the Sacramento location. Instead of dealing with the renovations after the fact, I'd get in from the ground up on the San Diego construction.

After verifying information on each sheet, then looking over the bar invoices and matching numbers to the inventory lists, I moved on to requests for permit updates. I ended up taking some aspirin to help get me through because otherwise, all of this would've laid me out.

Knowing I needed my friend to help with some of these because he'd been the one to walk me through them initially, as well as a couple of other people in the area, I shot a text and went back to working through the remaining pile of paperwork.

"You wanted to talk in person?" A knock sounded on my doorframe.

I looked up to see my frat brother and long-time friend dressed to the nines. I smiled then rose and walked around my desk to clap him on his back. Another day had passed and my headache was all but gone, so I figured I could have a couple of conversations in one setting.

Cantrell and I usually got together and chatted about what we'd been up to, but feeling like it would be wrong to have this conversation without our third musketeer, I suggested we head down Da Block. To be honest, I could use caffeine and sweets.

I'd persuaded him to drive because while I felt one hundred percent better than I did when I left the club after Leilani's house a few nights ago, I still got a little dizzy behind the wheel.

After waiting in the long line that stretched part of the way out the door of Sugar Crystal, we were finally greeted by our frat brother who stood behind the counter, finishing up with the customer. He waved us off to the side before joining us once he'd washed his hands.

"What are y'all doing in here near closing?" Midnight asked. "Don't you have businesses to run or women to bed?"

"It's always good to take a night off to recover, buddy," Cantrell said before pulling him into a half-hug and clapping him on the back.

I'd met both of them when we pledged during college. We ended up taking a few of the same classes, but our frat life was what really brought us together.

As young and impulsive teenagers, we went and got the insignia tatted on our shoulders to show our devotion. We were laughed at for weeks. It only bonded our brotherhood all the more. While we stayed in contact with more of the other men from our chapter, the three of us were the tightest.

"Let me grab your orders real quick," Midnight said.

Alanya waved him off and gave us a thumbs-up.

"Or not." He came toward us. "Looks like it'll be over in a minute."

"Damn, we should've invited her favorite person," Cantrell said. "Haven't caught up with Demontré in a while. Plus, the two of them in the same area is always a fun affair."

"You better chill before she kicks your ass," I said. "Justice says she's a fighter."

Seeing my sister's bridesmaid in here tripped me out every time. While she was a cool person, I never realized they were close enough for her to be included in the wedding like that. Alanya was extremely quiet as far as I could remember, but if Justice asked her to be in her affair, she had to be better friends with her than I thought.

"What's this impromptu meeting about?" Cantrell asked as we took a seat at one of the few empty tables in the corner.

"I asked if you'd oversee the changes I needed in the San Diego location I acquired," I said. "Are you down to do that for Sacramento as well?"

"Money is money, my friend, and traveling up and down

California is always worth it," Cantrell said. "The honeys be flocking."

I tried rolling my eyes, but the action caused the headache to flair. A few moments later a piping hot hazelnut mocha appeared in front of me. I thanked Alanya, who'd brought it and my banana zucchini loaf before she gave Cantrell his basic coffee and blueberry scones.

"Mention that dumb ass older frat brother of yours in my presence again and this coffee will be all over your lap." She tilted Cantrell's cup ever so slightly. "Do you understand?"

He jumped a little in his chair. "Yes, got it. Sorry. I was kidding."

She pursed her lips and looked him over before huffing and walking back to help the other clerk finish taking orders.

"Okay, she's legit a little reckless," Cantrell said.

"I told you don't fuck with her and that interior decorator," I said. "He's a sore spot for her for some good reason I don't know."

We all nodded before Midnight leaned his elbows on the table. "Why do I need to be part of this conversation or the one before this?" he asked.

"Can't I catch up with my boys?" I asked.

"Not unless something's wrong, and I'd been avoiding saying it, but you look like shit," Cantrell added.

"Getting over the flu. I don't feel that bad anymore, but damn if my head don't want to explode."

"You brought your sick into my ride, dude?" Cantrell asked.

"No, I'm not contagious anymore. I'm over it, just a water-filled noggin now."

"I swear if I get sick, I'm going to kick your ass. I've got a date tomorrow."

"Don't you always?" Midnight teased before turning his

attention back to me. "I've got a shoot coming up in a few days, gotta head to Reno, his little friend is coming with—"

"You messing with the lingerie queen?" I asked and he shrugged.

"Rumor don't want nothing from him but his assistance." Cantrell spoke around his scone. "Because he's my friend and both of y'all know her, he doesn't charge her full price."

"You mad because you haven't made a move after all these years and she's seeing which of us is the better brotha." Midnight puffed out his chest.

"Alright, alright. We not going down that hole again. Rumor don't want either of y'all asses. Let's leave it at that before she got y'all fighting for the umpteenth time," I said. "My head hurt too much for y'all nonsense."

I took a hearty sip and nearly burned my tongue off. After a moment to make sure I still had tastebuds, I changed the subject. "How's your mom?"

Midnight leaned back in his seat, crossing his arms.

"Declining," he sighed. "But she's still trying to be here as much as she can. I've pretty much canceled most of the things I had planned for the next couple of months so I could stay around and help her here. Beyond this thing with Rumor, I'm going to be fully running the bakery while Mom's doing her doctor's appointments."

"Awh, man. Sorry, man," Cantrell said. "If there's anything we can do you know we will."

Midnight nodded then got back to his feet. "It's on the house this time. Dawg life." He howled. We responded then he walked off to see to the last of the customers who'd entered the bakery.

"If it's alright with you, can we stick around 'til closing? I need to ask y'all about something."

"This have to do with a particular slightly older and

definitely don't want to be bothered with you lady friend?" Cantrell asked.

I didn't respond, instead, I ate some of my loaf.

"I figured as much. Overheard a conversation the other day about said woman. Sounds like someone's daydreaming about you, my dude."

"What did you hear?" I sat up bone-straight.

"I was in here while Missouri was picking up her normal baker's dozen and she was on the phone. Said something about Lani being moody and mopey since he left but trying to hide it by burying her nose in wedding stuff."

I rolled my neck side to side and let out a breath. "I'll explain the whole thing with her." *Maybe not the whole thing.* "It's not what you're probably thinking so gon' take your mind out the gutter."

"Sure, okay. Well anyway, I was with Rumor earlier. She said you asked her about helping you out with something to do with dress fittings?"

"Yeah, I'll tell you about it more once Midnight gets his Black ass back over here."

"While we wait, I got a question for you then," Cantrell said around a mouth full of his scone.

"Shoot." I drank some of my coffee, hoping the caffeine would help this damn migraine.

"What are we doing for your birthday this year? It's right around the corner and usually, we've planned out the location, how many chicks we going after and so much more."

I shot him a look before swallowing. "I'm planning this damn wedding. I forgot all about my birthday."

"It's your quarter-century year, that big two-five. You gotta do something. You know what? Don't worry about it, I got you."

"Oh hell. Don't plan some ignorant shit, Trell."

His mischievous smile told me it was going to be a mess. We switched gears and started talking about ideas for the San Diego club while we waited for Midnight to close up. I definitely needed both of their advice on how to move forward.

Should I be asking single dumbasses who stayed with someone as short a time as I had? Probably not. But my choices were slim and I knew they'd always give me the straight truth whether I liked it or not.

CHAPTER NINETEEN

LEILANI

"Pop, I have to ask you an important question." We had just finished our early breakfast.

It was seven in the morning, and we both had work later. The event for the publisher started just before noon, so I had to make sure everything was ready to go. He had a lecture hall that started at 10:15 a.m., so he needed to be at the school early enough to set up for his first class. I couldn't lollygag even if I wanted to.

"Well, that sounds ominous." My dad, ever the jokester, liked to lighten every mood when it seemed like it could turn dark or go bad.

"Seriously, Pop."

He nodded his head but kept the smile plastered on his face. "Okay, sweetie. I get it. What's got you all bent out of shape?"

"I want to know why you never remarried or started dating after mom died."

His mood instantaneously shifted. The easy-going smile was replaced by a sad frown. His beautiful brown eyes lost a bit of their gleam. I felt bad for bringing it up because we seldom talked about her death. We celebrated her birthday every year and went to visit her grave on the day she died, but didn't say much beyond a prayer and a memory.

Because both days were around Thanksgiving, that was usually a hard time for us. With Mother's Day in a few weeks, I thought it best to try to be a little more positive this year. If I could get answers on this, it would help me cope with her loss more, but also it might assist in how I viewed relationships.

"Baby, the main reason is that I am still in love with your mother, but beyond that, I didn't feel right starting up something new. I adore your mom and I feel like it would tarnish her memory if I remarried or even if I started seriously dating," he said. "I'm happy, though. You know, she was my soulmate, right? When it's my time to join her, I won't leave anyone behind but our beautiful girl to carry on our legacy."

A few tears escaped the corner of my eye. I sniffled and he smiled at me. "What's all this about? Why ask about that?"

"I'm so confused. I've always felt like you were happy on your own, so I didn't need anyone either." I wiped my face. "Like mom was such a strong, beautiful, shining star and when she died, we both lost someone important. I didn't want to ever feel like that again so I didn't want to make friends or get into a relationship out of the fear of losing the person."

"Oh, sweetie." He pulled me into his side. "I never wanted you to feel like that. Me not dating or marrying again shouldn't have stopped you from finding your happiness. If you hadn't noticed, you have a great group of friends who have supported you, even when you've been a complete little shit."

"Pop," I whined. He laughed.

"Let's be honest, you're my child. I know how horrible I

can be sometimes," he said. "Since you were raised by me, that rubbed off on you. A lot. Quiet and shy to the most but a WMD when pushed to a point."

"Okay, I get it." I sniffled as I wiped my eyes again.

"I'm just saying. Since your mom died, you became closed off to the world, but a few people weaseled their way in," he said. "Christopher did it best. That kid didn't care how much you tried to shoo him away when you were children. Honestly, I thought y'all were going to end up together."

I exaggerated gagging. He lightly shoved my shoulder. "You guys became joint at the hip. What was I supposed to think?"

"I don't know, maybe that girls and guys can have platonic relationships since you've pointed out that I've definitely made friends."

"Okay, well. I'm stating my case. I thought y'all were going to be an item. Honestly, I never saw you bring anybody home. Then you met Justice and Missouri. I was like, oh my. My baby likes the pretty ones, except you know, back then Zuri was—"

"Different, I know. Moving on."

"I wasn't going to say anything out of line. You know me better than that. She's as beautiful now as she was then. I for sure thought you and Justice were a thing, though," he said. "You spent so much time talking about her and then the three of you moved in together. I met her parents and everything."

I stared at him, my head tilted.

"Don't give me that look, your mother used to do the same thing whenever I said something a little dense."

I finally responded, raising an eyebrow before I spoke. "Maybe I don't know how this friend thing works, but don't people introduce them to their parents so folks know who they're hanging out with?"

"Yeah, I guess, but beyond Christopher, you'd never brought anyone around. So, I thought—"

"Never even experimented, Pop."

"Okay, okay." He pumped his hands toward me. "I'll move on."

"Please do, this awkward, late, half birds and the bees conversation is not what I wanted to be talking about."

His grin matched mine as he picked up where he left off.

"You formed your circle. Those three, but you can't discount the people you met because of them," he said. "Mercedes, Chance, Tristan, plus Justice's family, Missouri's aunt, and Chris's kids. You've let people in even if you haven't realized it. They all love you for you."

I hadn't ever thought about it. I'd been so focused on keeping men at bay—even after the few I'd messed around with, including Alexander—that I didn't realize I'd formed these strong bonds. I'd realized I'd made friends, sure, but not how my dad was describing it. These people cared about me and accepted all of my flaws, external and internal. One thing hit me like a brick the more I thought about it, though.

"I don't think I love any of them. I love you, Pop, but with them, I have strong feelings of adoration. To be completely truthful, I don't think I can love anyone else."

"You would do anything for them, wouldn't you?" he asked.

I sipped my coffee and shifted on the couch. I wasn't sure how to answer, but I guessed I would. I mean, I didn't know for sure, but it sounded like I might.

"Maybe," I mumbled.

"You told me you're planning a wedding for Justice even though she asked you to do it with her brother. That pissed you off from the start, right?"

I dramatically rolled my eyes before setting the mug back on the table next to my empty plate.

"That's love. It comes in all shapes, forms, and sizes. You want them happy just like they want the same for you," he said. "Each of you cares about the others in your different ways. It works, because if it didn't, you definitely wouldn't still be living together after all these years."

I smiled softly. "I don't think I can do the relationship thing, though. A few dates were me testing the waters, but none went beyond two and those were for all the wrong reasons."

"Sometimes you have to get your rocks off."

"Eww, Pop. Please don't go there."

He chuckled. I did not. It was not a mental image I wanted, but it made me a little curious.

"Since we're talking about my relationships and stuff," I said. "Why haven't I ever seen you hanging out with your professor buddies or whatever at any point since I was a kid?"

"I spent time with a couple of lady friends for purposes off and on, but usually when you had things to do so I made sure you were taken care of," he said. "Never in our house did anything happen before you even ask. As far as buddies, well me and some of the other professors have lunch or coffee together now and then. Most of them are married with kids, so I don't spend that much time with them."

"And you're truly happy being by yourself?" I watched his face carefully. "Living like this?"

"Yes, baby girl. I promise you, I'm fine. Beyond the occasional urge, I don't feel a pull toward anyone, and I'm content."

"Wouldn't Mom want you to find love again?"

"Maybe, but she can yell at me once I join her."

"This is why I don't…" Mumbling to myself, I scooped up my mug and drank down the last of my coffee before it went completely cold.

"Based on this conversation, it sounds like you are starting to like someone, and don't know how to feel," he said. "I'm going to offer you some advice."

I kept my focus on the now empty cup.

"You are still relatively young, and I never wanted you to be on your own. My hope for you was to always find your happiness; to find your forever," he said. "So, whoever this person is who has you wondering, who has you confused, whoever it is that has caused you to ask me these questions, maybe you should give it a shot with them. Obviously, this is a big first for you, and without even trying, you'll never know what could come of it."

"I don't know, Pop. It's complicated."

I slumped into the cushion and closed my eyes. This was the first day when quick or dramatic movements didn't make my head spin or my stomach lurch immediately. I'd say I was almost back to being A-okay.

"How is it complicated?"

"For starters?" I glanced at him. "They are younger, a lot younger."

"In the words of Aaliyah, 'age ain't—'"

"Don't say it, Pop."

He laughed and grabbed my hand. "If they are over eighteen, go for it, baby. I was eight years older than your mother, remember? I'd like to amend the age. Let's at least do old enough to drink. If he or she is at least twenty-one, give them a shot."

I nodded my head, unable to look at him again. Things I didn't want to think about, people I didn't have time for, were taking over my mind. I didn't want a relationship. Or did I?

"This has to be one of the weirdest conversations we've ever had," I said. "That's saying a lot because you were the one who taught me how to insert a tampon."

He shuddered. "Yeah, so glad that's over."

I gave him a big hug. He returned the embrace warmly.

"I love you, Pop."

"I love you too, sweetie. Everything will work out fine, I promise."

CHAPTER TWENTY

LEILANI

ON MY WAY to the office, I finally heard from the man who wouldn't leave my thoughts.

ALEXANDER: Hey, I'm sorry I haven't been in touch all week. I had to do a lot of traveling up and down the coast, cramming much of it into the last two days. I did end up under the weather and with things happening at all my nightclubs, I had to jump on them to get stuff handled as quickly as I could.

Alexander: I'm hoping you are feeling much better than you were last Friday. Also, I wanted to check if we were still on for our plans. According to the information you sent the dresses are coming along. They should be at a stage where we can check them out. I went ahead and double-checked with the boutiques that we still had appointments. Will I see you there?

Me: I'm fine, thanks. Hope everything is okay with your clubs, and yeah, I'll be there.

Alexander: I'll see you in the morning. We can go for

breakfast or I can cook for you again.

Me: Missouri and Tristan will be here. We can go out. I wouldn't want to wake them.

Alexander: I don't mind cooking for everyone, but whatever makes you happy.

Me: I'll meet you out front around nine o'clock, we can grab something on the way.

Alexander: Okay, See you then.

I COULDN'T FOCUS TOO much on him. After I chatted with my dad, I felt a little better. Maybe he and Mercedes were right. I should just let things progress. I should take charge and say something. For now, I had to make it through the last-minute things for this campaign.

The author was having an event at a local bookstore. The publisher decided it should not only be live, but we needed a transcript to roll on the screen. That was fine and dandy, except, it meant assuring things were adjusted in the social media campaign. It also meant getting someone who could pull together captions beyond the book chapters being read. The Q&As would be the most important part.

We could have an AI do it, but last time the words were all messed up. I didn't want that disaster again. It was fine, I wasn't sticking around for the whole event this time.

I had the rescheduled non-date to prep for on top of the other things Alexander and I planned to accomplish this weekend. The most important task was a progress report on the dresses. We were closing in on two-and-a-half months after the designs were started, and the girls wanted updates.

Since time was dwindling, we bumped the cake design situation to this week. I figured we could go about finalizing the plans for the bachelorette party with Missouri sometime before we went out next weekend. We'd need to put the deposit down for the bus or whatever we went with as soon as possible.

Beyond that, if we had time, we could continue our search for a caterer and see what else was left to take care of. Luckily, the binder had a lot of information. We just had to double-check certain details with the brides. But making smaller choices was on us. Unfortunately, they wanted the cake to be one of those choices. That wasn't small. That felt like a lot of pressure, but I knew we'd figure out something perfect for them.

AT NINE ON the dot Saturday morning, there was a knock on the front door. I went to open it and found Alexander standing there in the black button-down just like my first dream. He had the white slacks and suspenders to match. My shuddering gasp should have embarrassed me, but I couldn't believe my eyes. Was I dreaming again? He kicked off the wall and walked inside, the smile the same and everything.

My heart started beating fast, and I wasn't sure what in the fresh hell was happening. I glanced down, seeing a thigh-length cotton dress and flats, not jeans and a t-shirt, so unless the dream had changed, I was wide awake.

"What are you doing up here?" My voice came out shaky. "I told you I'd be down around now."

He closed the door behind him and cut toward the dining room. "Follow me."

Slowly, I made my way toward the kitchen, looking down the hall before crossing the threshold. This felt very similar to my dream, and I didn't know what to make of it. There were differences but I still had an eerie feeling about all of this. Alexander sat a bag on the table and started unloading it as I entered and leaned against the small piece of wall at the entrance.

"I thought I'd do the in-between thing and get us take-out from the little specialty place further up Da Block from Sugar Crystal," Alexander said. "I grabbed something for Missouri and Tristan as well, that way they can eat when they wake up."

Walking over to the table, I took a seat but kept my eyes on him. "I'm sure something quick from the bakery would've sufficed, thank you for this though. What's with the champagne?"

I remembered that from multiple dreams and had to actively keep my mind off the one from last night where he lapped it up from between my—

"Mimosas." A smirk adorned Alexander's annoyingly beautiful face, and I wanted to kiss him. I tamped that down fast.

"Ever since the blood orange ones we had down in Paso Robles, I've been craving another," Alexander said. "I'm not as good as them, but I've picked up a few things from my head bartender. I think I can make you a pretty mean one."

"Oh, okay," I said. "We burned so much daylight the last time we drank, though."

"That's why I'll make sure we keep it to a one-drink morning. Maybe later we can have a couple of variations."

"Don't hold your breath." The words may have held venom, but I could hear the smile on my face without even feeling it.

"So, I wanted to make you a meal," he said.

"What?" I interrupted him because this was definitely how all the dreams went.

He stopped making the second mimosa as he looked up at me, his confusion scrunching the entirety of his face before whatever he saw on mine made him chuckle.

"I wanted to make you a meal, but I didn't want to wake them," he said. "I figured this was the best of both worlds. I still get you to myself, but I didn't have to cook."

My heart raced in my chest as I eyed him suspiciously, but I couldn't ask for any further explanation because I wasn't sure I wanted to know what he meant. We ate in relative silence, the only conversation being me asking why he hadn't told me he'd gotten sick.

I knew he had, but that wasn't the point. Alexander's excuse, he stayed and bed and his phone had long since died by the time he thought to even check it days later. Just before we finished our meal, a sleepy Tristan walked in yawning followed by Missouri who rubbed her eyes ferociously.

"What's that delightful smell?" she asked.

"Alexander brought breakfast for all of us." He looked at me when I said his full name. "Dig in. Have him make you guys a mimosa as well. They're delicious."

WHEN WE ARRIVED at the dress shop in Russian Hill, I wasn't really comfortable going in. Not only was this neighborhood entirely more upscale than I preferred, but it was also a little snobby and didn't particularly cater to plus-sized women.

I mean, I had to look for bridesmaids' dresses in both stores to find something that looked great on four different-sized people. Dread wasn't even the right word for this.

I wished I'd dragged Missouri along because she took no-nonsense and would've been great at picking stuff out. I would have to make do with just Alexander. Thankfully, when we went inside, he took the lead.

"We're here to check on the progress of the dresses for

Chance Emerson and Justice Rutherford." He said to the woman standing at the reception desk.

"Of course, may I have your names?" She responded.

"Alexander Rutherford and Leilani Mitchell," he said. "We have the 10:25 appointment."

She nodded and looked at her computer. "Got it, please have a seat in the dressing room area. Leonard will be over in just a few minutes to meet with you. Will they be tried on?"

How in the hell would that happen, lady? Do you see Chance or Justice? No. I trained my face to remain unfazed when Alexander nodded his head.

"Rumor Lovelace should be here in the next ten minutes," he said. "She'll be trying on both dresses."

"Noted," the receptionist said. "Thank you, please go take a seat."

When we arrived in the mirror-filled dressing room, I looked at Alexander and raised an eyebrow, waiting for an explanation. When he returned the expression, I wanted to punch him. He could be so exasperating, but this wasn't the time for it.

"Rumor?" I asked.

I hoped the annoyance wasn't etched across my face. It had to be the same one from all those years ago. That wasn't a very common name. Plus, I'd heard it a couple of times in passing from either him, Cantrell or Midnight.

He nodded. "Yeah. She's a friend."

I worked to remain calm. Maybe I was overreacting, but she had called him in the middle of the night all those years ago. That seemed extremely friendly to me. Not just the norm, but the bang buddy type.

"Listen," Alexander said, shifting in his seat. "We never talked about that night. You need to know—"

He stopped mid-sentence because Rumor walked into the room. Well, I could only assume who she was, because damn if she wasn't gorgeous. About the same height as both brides and favoring their bodies almost exactly, I sighed and looked down at my feet.

"Hi everyone, I'm Leonard," A slender man swooped into the area moments later. "I'm the designer for the beautiful Ms. Emerson and her lovely bride-to-be, Ms. Rutherford. Chance's gown isn't at a stage to be tried on, but this one is almost an exact size replica, although it doesn't have the adornments because each is a one-of-a-kind dream."

He held up a see-through wardrobe bag and twirled it. "Anyway, I can show you the progress of the dress, but again it is not ready to be tried on. Justice's on the other hand is basically done. That one can be worn, but I have to beg you to be extremely careful. A stylist can assist in getting it on if need be. Actually, I'll have to demand that."

"That'll be fine. This is Rumor, she'll be trying on both dresses," Alexander said. "This is Leilani, the maid of honor, and I'm Alex, the man of honor."

Leonard nodded and showed Rumor where to get changed. He called for a stylist to come assist her, then he walked over to me. "Okay, missy. You have to get a look at some bridesmaids' dresses, right?"

Leonard's too-chipper demeanor was making me nauseous again. I had no energy to deal with him. Plus, I was getting angrier by the minute. This whole thing with Rumor being here was pissing me off.

But, why did I even care? Beyond the fact that I wished I'd known someone was trying on my best friend's dress, Alexander and I weren't actually together. He was entitled to be around whomever he wanted.

I'd ask him about it later, hopefully when I was much calmer than I felt at the moment. I rose to my feet and let Leonard walk me around the shop, pulling dress after dress from the racks that were either the style or the color Justice and Chance had in mind for us.

Trying on an off-the-shoulder, sweetheart bodice bridesmaid number made me miss what Rumor looked like in the gown similar to Chance's, but from what I could hear, she looked stunning.

If I'd stopped long enough, I could've joined them to admire the dress, but honestly, what was the point? In a month we'd be back here for her to try on the real thing plus, I didn't want to see Alexander ogling her.

After six dresses, I made a note of two that could work. Rumor tried on the second gown, which I actually did see because it would be the one Justice wore for the ceremony.

Rumor looked breathtaking, and to know we were about to go to this other shop to look for reception outfits made my stomach drop. Alexander appreciated the way she looked. I could tell that from the expression he gave when she stepped up on the platform.

When we finally arrived at the second location, Rumor tried having a conversation with me, but I had no energy for it. I behaved as nicely as I could, but all I wanted was to go home and eat a tub of Rocky Road, and I didn't even like ice cream like that.

I was being childish, which only made me feel silly. I couldn't stop it, though.

The associate brought a few dresses for me to try on. The first one was a halter top that cinched at the waist. It was floor-length and flowed out from mid-thigh down. It was easy to walk in and looked really nice. She asked me to walk around the dressing room to show it to the others I was with. I didn't want to, but I'd rather not argue.

"That looks amazing on you," Rumor said. I smiled and stared at myself in the mirror.

Through the reflection, I saw Alexander's eyes on me.

When his gaze reached mine, there was something there I couldn't put my finger on. He slightly shook his head, a small smile playing on his lips.

"You look stunning, sweetheart," Alexander said.

I turned around to glare at him. It was one thing for him to call me that in private or in front of my friends, but I didn't know Rumor and I was confused by what the hell was going on between them. When I caught her eye, she smiled.

Wait, what? She was standing there in a potential dress for Chance. She looked gorgeous, but he hadn't paid her any mind since I walked out. His eyes remained on me, even right now.

"He's not wrong," she said. "You look phenomenal."

"Thank you," I said, my shoulders dropping. "You look beautiful, too."

She smiled and almost curtsied. I needed to talk to Alexander. This was confusing. The associate shuffled both me and Rumor off to try on more dresses. Each time I came out, he spoke toward Rumor about what she was wearing but kept his eyes on me.

After narrowing down dress options with suggestions from Rumor, she said goodbye and we headed off to the bakery. There were three more things to get through with the amount of time left in the day—one of those was talking to him about her.

CHAPTER TWENTY-ONE

ALEXANDER

"Appointment for the Rutherford/Emerson engagement," I said as we reached the woman behind the counter at the cakery.

She smiled softly before looking at a booklet off to her side. "Yes, I see. I'll grab the chef for you. Please, have a seat in the far-right booth. She'll be out in a few minutes."

I pulled out Leilani's chair and she sat down. She looked like a lot was on her mind, but this wasn't the time to talk. I knew seeing Rumor upset her, but the drive from the dress shop to here wasn't long enough for us to have a conversation about that.

I needed to make it clear now—before anything bad could happen—that Rumor was a friend. A mutual one for the most part, but a friend and nothing more. Since we likely had a couple of minutes before the chef would come out, I thought I could reassure her now. But when I took the spot beside Leilani, a woman in a color-block dress and baker's shoes came walking out from behind the counter.

"I'm Chef Amanda. Nice to meet you both. What a lovely couple. Let me guess, you're Justice," She looked at me as she finished shaking my hand. "Which would make you Chance?"

Leilani's amazing chocolate skin turned a raspberry blush before she shook her head.

"No, he's Alex and I'm Leilani. Justice is his sister and my best friend. We're helping the couple out because work called," she said. "I thought it had been noted we were coming instead of them?"

Did she just call me Alex? Interesting. Chef Amanda sat down embarrassed and started looking through the thick three-ring binder she'd placed on the table. I glanced at Leilani, a look passed between the two of us, but I didn't say anything. That would be something else I'd bring up later. For now, we had to focus on the design for this cake.

"My apologies. I hadn't actually met them in person because they knew exactly what cake flavors they wanted, and I'd spoken primarily with a planner. Somehow I forgot that it was too brides as well. Apologies." Chef Amanda rubbed her finger down the page before tapping it. "I see right here that y'all were coming. Okay, so do we know all the details the couple wants and needs? This includes budget, inspiration images, wedding style, etc."

"We have everything." Leilani pulled her tablet from her purse and unlocked it. Her business persona turned on. "And you're right, Justice and Chance have already chosen flavors, but everything else is up to us. We have a budget and—"

If I could choose one thing I loved about Leilani, it was this. *Love.* There was that word again. But the confidence that shined through every time she took control and got things up and running was something to behold.

I sat back and watched as they talked logistics from the range of the budget to the date needed, the venue, the number of guests, and the time of day. Chef Amanda was more than happy to drive the cake to the southern tip of

California, which she said she recalled speaking to Justice about a month and a half earlier.

I wasn't sure Leilani knew she had a glow when she was in business discussions, but I could sit back and watch this forever. I left her to handle this while I checked in with Rumor. I needed to thank her for stepping in. Since she and my sister were virtually the same size, I ran it past both brides to see if they were cool with having the dresses tried on.

They'd loved the idea and Rumor had a bit of free time in between gigs, so it worked out perfectly.

RUMOR: Cantrell said how much you needed my help. You know the three of y'all have always gotten on my nerves, especially since I started my business, but I'll always do whatever I can to assist.

Me: Cantrell had to convince you? Damn. Well, either way, thanks. I guess he is your best non-boyfriend friend after all.

Rumor: Y'all gotta stop with that. We have never and will never mess around. Drop it already. Lol. Speaking of…

Rumor: The adorable woman you were with, that's your sister's best friend, right? The one you used to salivate over every time you got drunk and started talking about who you wished you had?

Me: That's none of your business. Bye, Ru. Thanks.

SHE SENT a gif of someone keeling over from laughter, and I stuck my phone back in my pocket before rejoining the conversation. Both women sitting with me were looking at me. I'd missed something which evidently annoyed Leilani.

"Your sister's favorite flavor?" The chef asked.

"Black Forest cherry torte. She's been in love since, well since I was a kid, but probably before that too."

A smile warmed Leilani's face. "You do pay attention to women you don't want to sleep with, look at you, kid," she said. "Thanks for confirming Justice's flavor."

"First, eww. Following my statement about my sister's cake choice with sex is gross, and second, I know a lot about a lot. Want to know your favorite?" I leaned toward her and surprisingly she didn't back down.

"I know what I like, *Alex*, I don't need you to remind me."

There she went saying my name like that again.

"Coconut with shaved chocolate and strawberry filling," I inched closer to her, our mouths less than a foot apart. "When it's warm outside, you'll pair it with a glass of sparkling wine. Rosé typically."

She swallowed as her eyes dropped to my mouth before lifting her gaze back to mine. The slight part of her lips allowed me to see how deep she inhaled before she got ready to speak.

"Are you two an item as well?" Chef Amanda broke the moment.

I wanted to toss her binder across the room. That's the most reaction I'd gotten out of Leilani since we had breakfast this morning and this woman had to open her big mouth. With the intensity gone, Leilani cleared her throat and refocused the conversation on tasting options.

I took a deep breath, leaned back in my seat and brought my attention away from the edge of the near kiss we could've shared. One that would've been on her terms because she'd said no mouths touching, but this seemed to be something she wanted.

"Chance wants Strawberry Rhubarb, and the combination of the two doesn't work, but if we do four layers, they both get what they want," Leilani said. "Their keepsake tier can be vanilla with filling from both. I think they'd love that."

I was only able to nod because words would betray me. I wanted to taste something, but it wasn't cake. Chef Amanda noted the request and then went off to grab slices of three flavors. Leilani must've told her the ladies wanted us to eat cake for fun.

Luckily, the cakery made them regularly, even though two of the choices were summer favorites. She returned to the table with six forks and three plates. A second person brought over napkins and two glasses of water.

"We can start with the vanilla, but do know, my cakes are complex in flavor and never basic or simple. I use buttermilk for my standard flavors to enhance the richness of each ingredient." The chef said as Leilani scooped a forkful into her mouth.

The moan had my fingers twitching. I wanted to chase the cake down her throat, tasting the remnants on her lips and tongue as I pulled her into my lap and found my way under that obscenely thin cotton camisole dress she'd put on.

Fighting the sudden urge to lose my damn mind, I filled my mouth with the cake as well. Flavors burst on my tastebuds. I had to ignore my urge to groan louder than she had.

"Right?" Leilani's breath tickled my cheek as I opened my eyes to find her in my personal space. "It's amazing. I might have to get a little cake just because."

Chef Amanda smiled before directing us to sip the water and move on to the next flavor. Similar reactions lifted out of both of us, but her more than me because I wasn't big on rhubarb.

For the most part, I'd been able to avoid it whenever Chance brought it around. The compote wasn't my thing when it came to the dessert, but I said they would enjoy it and quickly drank down part of the remaining liquid in my glass.

I very much enjoyed the complexity of the last dessert, partly because every birthday Justice had at home was signed with this cake. The whipped cream with sliced cherries paired delightfully with the liveliness of the chocolate, coconut, and buttermilk flavors. This was something I could see at my wedding if I ever had one.

I shook my head as I ate another bite before feeling pressure at the side of my mouth. Opening my eyes, I found Leilani licking icing from the pad of her thumb.

"Baby boy eats like a toddler. Had to get that little bit of mess you made," she smirked. "All better now."

I don't think I'd ever seen her look at me like that before. I swallowed, but I couldn't even comment. Leilani had left me floored. Her attention went back to the chef and they continued discussing in detail how they would go about design, size, and more. I gave my input on occasion, but for the most part, I remained quiet and nodded my head at the appropriate time.

Her 180 demeanor change since leaving the dress shops had me working to keep up, especially because this felt like more of a body swap situation than an attitude switch, but I couldn't say anything until I got her back to the privacy of the club at minimum. Once we'd finished detailing everything, this part, I'd tuned into, we said our goodbyes and decided to have an early meal before doing the last thing that would be on the list.

This was the date part of the weekend's events. I'd been waiting to get her alone since I walked into the apartment last Friday. The table wasn't as private as the one I'd booked before, but it still offered a semi-romantic setting and gave me a gorgeous view of her in the dimmed red light.

"We didn't have to have a sit-down dinner. We could've

grabbed something to go." Leilani pointed out after we'd placed our order.

"Spend all day with such a beautiful woman and not treat her to a real meal?" I asked. "That's quite rude, wouldn't you say? Plus, we missed our date last week, so I'd like to think of this as catching up for the lost time."

She dropped her body back against the chair and turned her nose up at me. I felt the comment coming. She'd probably finally thought back to Rumor. I didn't want to talk about that just yet, so I stopped her.

"I know what you're going to say. This isn't a date, blah blah blah," I said. "I can make it feel less romantic if you like? How about I get down beneath this tablecloth and show you how you could be worshiped? I can be the man on his knees having you panting in that seat or we can sit here and enjoy our food, then go work on choosing a cocktail for the wedding."

A breath rushed out of her before she gripped the sides of the table and brought herself up to a straighter position. With a shaky hand, she grabbed the glass of water the server had brought over and drank part of it.

"I thought so. Now, there's something I'm sure you've been thinking about off and on all day. Rumor, right?"

"Isn't that the same woman from—"

"Yes. She's Cantrell's best friend. I wasn't messing with her back then and I'm not messing with her now. Do you believe me?"

Leilani huffed but said nothing. I was about to say something else, but my phone rang. Looking down I saw Ego's name. "If you'll excuse me, I have to take this."

Once I stepped outside, I called her back because I'd missed answering by seconds.

"I'll take you up on that offer, but I need some time to dot my I's and cross my T's," Ego blurted by way of hello.

"Alright, that'll give me time to get everything ready for you here. What do you need from me? You want a solo act or a group? Do you work well with others?"

"I've been choreographing for a few years. Recently, I'd say the people around me were coming for my head, so I don't know."

"We'll work on the details closer to your arrival," I said. "I've got a previous engagement I need to return to though, but I'll be in touch to smooth out the beginnings of our partnership."

Her pause had me checking the phone. "Okay, yeah. Thanks, Alexander."

"Call me, Alex. Talk to you soon."

Work felt smooth now that I could get all of my clubs going the way I wanted, just as long as she didn't back out. That meant my focus could lie on finishing up this wedding planning and showing Leilani I was indeed worth her time and the effort I'd been throwing at her.

The way she'd been behaving since I took care of her while she was sick was up and down, but definitely more responsive than ever before. I walked back toward our table, a hopeful feeling flooded my stomach and it felt weird because I'd never had that happen before.

Leilani looked up at me with a genuine smile as I took my seat.

"Work?"

I nodded. "If you want to know, I can tell you about it."

"Yes, please."

Surprised by her response, I went back to a previous conversation we hadn't finished because we were tired and sick. Now she could know all the details about what I planned to do with my clubs.

CHAPTER TWENTY-TWO

LEILANI

It had been a long day, but surprisingly, beyond the time spent around Rumor, I was fully enjoying myself. And honestly, she hadn't done anything wrong. I'd just felt a little intimidated. After Alexander said she was Cantrell's best friend, I felt lighter.

The few mentions I'd caught made more sense now, but regardless I'd overreacted earlier. And though I still had questions about why she'd called so late all those years ago, it wasn't my business or important.

Plus, he'd paid his attention to me, not her. Once we'd finished eating dinner, we headed over to Club Haze because he said we should make a signature drink for Chance and Justice to have at the bachelorette party, and another one for the wedding itself.

We arrived at the bar and sat in one of the VIP booths as one of his bartenders made us a series of drinks to try. Apparently, he'd also be the one to serve them on the party bus and at the reception, to make sure no mistakes would be made. The man seemed loyal to Alexander to a fault, and that made me wonder how great a boss he could be.

"This will be what? Drink number four?" I shouted over the music, making me have to get close to him.

Alexander's knuckles grazed my now bare shoulder because I'd taken off the cardigan I had on over my dress. The sensation zapped through me, but I chose to focus on what he said instead of how I felt.

"You axed the first three," he said. "Said they were too sweet, too strong or too fruity. Colin's going to try something a little different this time."

The heat from his mouth dancing against the edge of my earlobe set my skin ablaze. I had to fight to remember myself and why we were here. I needed to focus on what we were doing for the party and that's it.

Colin sat his next concoction in front of us, explaining what was in it and what the hints were that we tasted, but I couldn't exactly hear him over the music. I nodded anyway and sipped it. This one tasted nice but still didn't scream yes for me. Alexander watched to see what I'd say, but I hadn't decided how to respond so as not to annoy either man.

This was the only one I'd been fond of so far, but I knew he could make something to knock my metaphorical socks off. Between the wine at dinner and the half-drank cocktails in front of us, I was starting to feel the buzz. While they might not be the one, they were strong.

Colin sat another drink in front of me. His face shined with hope. I looked toward Alexander. He had an eyebrow lifted. He'd slowly started shifting closer and closer to me, but I didn't say anything. Not much space separated us anymore and I would've said something, but I didn't care.

On the contrary, I liked it. He was staking a claim, even if silently. It wasn't that I thought any man in this club, let alone Colin, would make a move while I sat here literally enraptured by Alexander, but it was kind of nice to know he was feeling a little possessive.

I raised the cup to my lips and took a sip. It was sour. I absolutely hated it, but my tastebuds didn't matter. I knew Chance and Justice wouldn't like it even more. I screwed my face up as the liquid slid down my throat, then shook the feeling from my whole body. When I trained my gaze on Colin again, he was damn near pouting.

"I'm sorry," I said. "That was just—"

'It's fine," Colin said. "Sours aren't everybody's thing. Thought I'd give it a shot."

Alexander lifted his glass to his lips and drank a bit. A tiny amount dripped down into his chin hair. I laughed and wiped his face before shaking my head. "It's not bad, but Leilani's right. It is very sour. My sister would hate it, too. Sorry, man."

Colin shrugged. "No worries," he said. "Let's try something else."

By the seventh drink, we finally had our winner. I asked if we could do a slight variation on it, allowing one version for the party bus and the other for the reception. Colin smiled and nodded.

I looked at Alexander and he was grinning. The name came to both of us simultaneously.

"Cravings," we said.

The cocktail was delicious and something you could want more than once. It had Maker's Mark and vanilla Crown Royal for its base, then was topped with ounces of Vanilla Coke and a cherry garnish. I don't know exactly how much of each thing was in it, but it was perfect, and it was delicious.

Colin made a second one with D'Ussé instead of whiskey and it was equally amazing. I added the word 'hidden' to the reception version and the name stuck. After finally getting the drink portion of our plans done, we moved upstairs to Alexander's office where we could discuss what else we needed to finish doing and hear without yelling ourselves hoarse. Once the door shut behind him, I'd already taken a seat on the very comfortable couch across from his desk.

"Alright, we have pretty much everything for the cake selected. We checked on the dresses. The florist has been taken care of." Alexander's words slurred a little, but he seemed coherent enough for the conversation to continue. "Justice and Chance already had the invitations made and sent out. What else we got done?"

"Wait, did we send off the wedding invitations?" I asked. "We need to keep track of the RSVPs."

He took his jacket off and sat it on a coat rack next to the door. The way his back flexed beneath his dress shirt was sending my mind places. It had been a while since we'd had sex, and between the way he'd assured me that I was important to the way this alcohol was making me feel, I wanted to act on the thoughts swirling around in my head.

"Yeah, I did it before I came by the house last weekend." He sat on the couch beside me. "After we looked over them and sent the pictures to Justice and Chance a few weeks back, they finally said everything looked good and I shipped them off."

I shook the thoughts from my mind. *Wedding planning first.* "Okay, perfect. So, I convinced Missouri to finally stop trying to be the photographer," I said. "On the list of things to do, did you see find one?"

"Yeah, I made a few calls and I'm waiting to hear back. Midnight and Missouri suggested a few people." Alexander took another sip of his drink. "What about the seating chart? On the spreadsheet, I didn't see any updates to that."

I drank a bit more of my cocktail. The longer I sat here in the confines of his office, the more I wanted to climb into his lap, but not yet. We needed to focus. Assuring the wedding stuff was on track was more important. Had I included the information for the seating chart?

"We still need to find the vendor for the chairs and tables before we can go about doing the seating," I said. "What about the centerpieces?"

"Haven't heard back in a few weeks," Alexander said. "I'll reach out on Monday. So, now that we've taken care of all that, what are we hopping on tomorrow?"

"Not sure yet, I think we might have a free day. So, tonight can I hop on something?" He almost spat out the end of his Hidden Cravings as I turned toward him.

The look on his face nearly made me laugh. He'd made his comment about climbing under a table during dinner, but me wanting to ride him was a surprise? Alexander sat his cup down and faced me. "What?"

"You said you would have me beggin'," I said. "I've yet to do that. I have demanded though. In this case, I'm suggesting. Maybe you can get me to beg for something this time."

I shrugged.

"I'm gon' give you what you asking for." Alexander remained in his spot, eyes darting across the edges of my face. "And I guaran-damn-tee you'll be begging for more before the night ends."

My eyebrow raised and a smirk crossed my face. I grabbed the collar of his shirt and pulled him to me. Our lips were a breath apart. I shouldn't kiss him. That would mean so much more, but I wanted to taste his lips. To remember how good they'd felt before.

I liked Alexander and I knew he liked me. Hopefully, this would tell him I was on board. Fuck the ground rules. I was willing to try. I pressed my lips to his. He went bone straight before melting into the kiss, his hands sinking into my hair. His hold kept me right where he wanted me as our mouths worked together.

The sound of the music below our feet faded. His nips and tongue flicks caressed my collarbone as he pulled the sleeve of my dress down my shoulder. Once we were naked, Alexander had the nerve to lean away. That earned him a growl from deep within my chest, but the look on his face made me sit up and question my greedy actions.

"Okay, maybe we shouldn't do this." I pulled back from him. "You look a little distressed."

"You're kidding me, right?" Alexander asked. "I've wanted you since I was fifteen. I've been perplexed by you since I was eleven."

"First off, eww. That's gross. You're killing the mood. You were a kid. Secondly, that doesn't change the fact that you look confused."

"Not gross because I'm not a kid anymore. If I want you, I can have you. This is more than mutual at this point, but you said no kissing. What changed?"

I stared into his eyes. He changed. He grew up. I got to see the product of now. The way he cared for me when I was sick. The way he handled business. The fact that he'd continued to stick around beyond the sex, and not just because of the wedding planning. I got to know him for him and not my thoughts of who he likely was because of what he used to do.

"You," I said. "I have feelings for you. I want to see where this can go."

Alexander looked shocked. There was no going back now. A smile graced his face before he nodded, then bent over to reach into his pants pocket. I watched as he pulled out his wallet, and then a condom. He'd been sure to keep one on him ever since Oceanside. It was both funny and cute, even though I'd done the same.

When he leaned over me and lowered us to the couch cushions, I rested my hands on his shoulders. I felt his muscles shift as he pressed his body to mine. He feathered kisses across my jawline and smoothed his hand up my side.

If nothing else, he knew the small things to do to get me in the mood. By the time he sank into me with such care and ease, I couldn't believe I'd shared my feelings. Did I regret it?

Not at all, especially when Alexander started moving in and out of me like he knew my body better than I did. His kisses became more loving and I felt myself building up. His hand tucked under my arm, grabbing my shoulder to hold me in place as his thrusts sent stars into my atmosphere.

"Fuck," I breathed against his mouth.

Reaching my hand between us, I rubbed my clit as he moved his head to watch the action.

"Shit, sweetheart," Alexander groaned. He rolled his hips, pushing deeper inside of me.

My legs started shaking, but I didn't want to come yet. "From the back, take it from the back."

I breathed.

Alexander paused to stare at me, a grin spreading across his face. After a beat, he slid out and leaned back so I could readjust. I stood and walked around him to lean over the arm of the couch. I perched my ass in the air and looked at him. He watched me for a long moment before he stood up and moved behind me.

"Never ceases to surprise me," Alexander whispered in my ear as he drove his fingers into my hair and pulled my upper body toward him. "I like this side of you."

When he sank back into me, he tightened his grip. One of his hands massaged my breast, playing with each as he filled me repeatedly. I moaned and threw my ass back at him, meeting him thrust for thrust. His teeth sank into my neck and my eyes melted closed. An intense feeling built in my stomach.

"Harder, Alex," I said just above a breath.

He let go of my hair, kissed my neck, and pushed me over the arm of the couch. His grip dug into my hips as he plunged into me with more force. I gripped the couch cushion and got up on my tiptoes angling him further inside.

Alexander pulled out and spun us around until he was seated and I was on his lap, impelled by his dick once more. Placing my hands on the table in front of me, I positioned myself so I could start bouncing on him.

A shuddering breath racked through me as my orgasm rocked through my body much faster than I thought. I felt myself falling, but he caught me and held me flush against him as I breathed through the violent aftershocks.

With my elbows resting on the table, I slowly opened my eyes. The vibration of his phone ringing grabbed my attention and I couldn't help but glance over.

Rumor's Cell and a photo of her lit up his screen. I pulled myself from his grasp and moved away, legs shaking.

CHAPTER TWENTY-THREE

LEILANI

"WHAT'S WRONG?" Alex asked. "Did I do something wrong?"

My eyes flew from him and fixed themselves on the phone beside me. He seemed to be working to take his mind off how we fucked. He couldn't focus on what was bothering me while his head stayed in that moment. By the time he looked at me, the vibration had ended and started up a second time.

"I'll call her back later. Can't be anything important."

"You sure? I mean, it is 11 p.m. on a Friday."

"It's not like that, Leilani," he said. "I'm not messing with her. I told you that already."

"I believed you when you said it," I said. "I just find it funny that after all the time I've known you, I never heard her name. Never randomly saw her with y'all either, then she shows up at the fittings. Cantrell's friend or not, she's fucking beautiful. You wouldn't want to fuck her? I damn sure would."

Getting his breath under control, he looked at me with an almost vehement disgust. "Do you hear yourself? I don't care what Rumor looks like, I'm not interested," Alexander said. "Why can't you see that I want you? I've only ever fucking wanted you."

"Because you were attentive earlier and now she's calling you on repeat in the middle of the night," I said, fists balling. "Not sixty seconds ago you were inside me. I told you I had fucking feelings for you. I think I have the right to ask about the beautiful ass female hitting you up on repeat."

As if I needed confirmation, his phone screen lit up again, Rumor calling once more. I waved my hand toward it. He huffed and shoved the device onto the floor.

"You never gave me the time of day, then we're stuck together for this shit. You decide we should start screwing," he shouted. "First you get all flirty, then you kissed me and we have sex. You let me get between your thighs whenever you or I wanted it, then you slept in my arms. You let me take care of you. I know you better than you think. You could've told me to kick rocks, but you wanted me to stay. Make that shit make sense, Lani."

I stared at him but said nothing.

"Exactly. You've wanted me for a long fucking time," Alexander said. "I have not shown interest in no one else but you, yet you wanna get pissy about someone calling? There's insecure and then there's you."

My open palm connected with his face before I stepped around him and snatched my dress from the ground, covering myself. I felt ever much like a fool. Refusing to let this arrogant prick make me cry, I worked to put my dress back on. "I knew this was a bad decision from the very beginning."

My phone flashed and buzzed as he started to apologize. Ignoring him, I pulled it free of my discarded purse to check who was calling.

"Hey," I said, drowning him out in the background. "Everything okay?"

"I should be asking that," Chance said. "What's going on?"

"Nothing," I sighed. "You good?"

"I was calling because I woke up and was checking my emails. I got one from Shadow's Peak a few days ago," Chance said. "They were confirming the cancellation of the space. What happened?"

My eyes grew. I spun around to stare at Alexander. "I'll call you back." I hung up before she could say anything else. "I didn't cancel the venue space, did you?"

I interrupted his continuous rant. He remained naked, half-limp dick resting against his thigh as he picked up his phone and started scrolling through it.

"Why would I cancel the space?" he asked. "That was the only thing that was absolutely mandatory for the wedding."

Alexander's eyes grew. He mumbled fuck under his breath. His head dropped as he held his phone out to me.

I grabbed it and read through the email from Monday.

Ms. RUTHERFORD AND Ms. EMERSON,

Thank you for considering Shadow's Peak as your wedding venue. We understand that situations arise. We hope that you think of us in the future for other events. We have canceled the date and are processing the refund of your deposit.

Thank you,
Maximo Ariana
General Manager

I DIDN'T GET that email. I was very confused. When I saw it had been forwarded by Chance twenty minutes ago, I realized she must've sent it to me too. Since they had initially booked it before their wedding planner, everything with the venue had gone through them instead of us.

"What happened?" I asked, tossing the phone on the couch beside Alexander.

"I don't know," he said. "I was sick as shit and in bed with you. I don't remember seeing an email or clicking anything."

"Fucking—" I sighed.

I had to try to fix this. I stuffed my phone back into my purse and grabbed my underwear from under his foot, tossing them in my bag because I was too enraged to pull them on.

"Shit," I muttered struggling with the zipper on my dress.

Alexander helped me, but I pushed him away because I didn't want him near me. Beyond his asshole comment about my insecurities, the wedding was more important. If we couldn't get the venue back, everything would be screwed.

"You gon' ahead and deal with your Rumor situation and I'll take care of the venue and everything else. I don't need your help any longer, I've got this," I said. "You screwing me or anything else up won't be helpful with the amount of time we have left. This shit has to be fixed now."

"I have three successful businesses and I'm working on a fourth. Unlike somebody else in this room, I don't work for someone else who doesn't want to see me move any further up the corporate chain," Alexander said. "There is no Rumor situation, but whatever. Go run back to your little reader cave and listen to what other people tell you to do."

I snapped my attention to him, ready to punch him in the face. He was pulling on his pants at the other end of the couch.

"And," he added, "I'm happy with the way I look and what I do for a living. I'm not some snail that hides in my shell whenever things get too hard or too scary," he said. "So go, go ahead, do you. I'm too tired of this. I could care fucking less."

What an asshole.

"Please do that. Please care fucking less." I fought angry tears. "I thought you were a shit when you were growing up. Even thought you'd changed, now I see you're still a fucking dick."

Snatching up everything that belonged to me, I stomped barefoot out of his office and toward the stairs. As I started my descent, I could partially hear his pleas.

"Leilani, wait! I'm sorry."

I didn't stop, nor did I turn to look.

"Lani." I felt the vibration of the steps as he came thundering down them behind me.

Pushing through the people on the dance floor, I knew I'd need to take a shower not only to wash his scent off me, but because the sticky substances from the hardwood were all over my feet, and someone dropped a drink that splashed my ankles and shins. Once I got outside, I hailed a cab. Thankfully, one was on the street.

"Lani, wait. Please, let me apologize. I'm sorry. I fucked up. I didn't mean what I said." Alexander's hands pressed against the window.

His shirt was splayed open and his belt rested limp, undone. If nothing else, everybody's different version of this would be all over the neighborhood before the sun rose. I shook my head.

"I've been trying to prove myself to you for four years. To show you that I'm not that little kid you used to know," Alexander said. "Calling you out on your job was wrong. I know you love what you do, but I see so much more potential in you. Please forgive me."

I looked at him through the glass, fighting back the urge to cry through the swirl of emotions I felt at the moment. No way was he being serious right now. Forgive him after the shit that he just said? For how all of this was going down right now?

This was why I preferred to read about love. It could be as messy as it wanted in a book. I would even feel for the characters, but experiencing it myself? *Wait! This wasn't love.* I liked him. I didn't love him. No…

"Rumor is my friend. Period. Nothing is going on between us. To be honest, I'm sure she and Cantrell are a thing and don't want to admit it," Alexander said. "I have no interest in her whatsoever. Please trust me. I've never lied to you. I've never led you astray. I would never play with your heart. I love you."

I stared at him as a weight settled on my chest. His eyes searched my face. There was a desperation in his gaze. I couldn't deal with this. Did he love me? *No.* Not possible.

I tapped the glass between the cabbie and me, asking him to pull off. Not looking back to see Alexander one last time, I made a vow to go back to what I'd been doing, living my life and making it through. I was done with him. My feelings would have to subside.

If I had to only see him for the wedding events, I could do that, but nothing could make me deal with him on any other level. Forget what Mercedes said, what my dad said. I was fine on my own. I didn't need love. I didn't need to put myself out there.

This was what I'd get. A snot-nosed asshole pointing out everything I'd ever felt some type of way about. These next few months might be difficult, but I'd make it through. I had a job I loved and I'd found something else I was interested in —event planning.

If nothing else, Alexander had taught me some stuff about myself. I was a strong, beautiful, confident woman. I should've known that already. I'd lived it. I'd breathed it, but until he pointed out what make me feel less than, I hadn't realized I'd been holding myself back. Fuck him, but I couldn't help but be grateful.

It was time to make some changes and that started with me.

CHAPTER TWENTY-FOUR

ALEXANDER

Fucking up never felt so bad. I tried to get Leilani to talk to me. I needed to properly apologize. To tell her I was being a dick and got defensive for... no reason at all.

I don't know why I responded like that. I felt attacked. Rumor calling again after we had sex that had changed our dynamics once more seemed to be a fucking thing for her. It was like she knew I was with Leilani and her radar said, "fuck shit up."

But that wasn't the case at all. Rumor attended Frisco State with Cantrell, Midnight, and me. She and Cantrell had known each other well before college. Beyond hanging out with her whenever he invited her along, I didn't know her like that.

The night she'd rung my line all those years ago had been the start of this barrier between Leilani and me. When Rumor called this time, it was because she was with Cantrell and Midnight when he found out his mother died. Rumor was calling so I could come over because Midnight wasn't doing well.

The first time she'd called was from the pre-graduation

party we'd been at. Cantrell was having issues with his diabetes and had drunk too much. She'd wanted to let me know he had to go to the hospital. Neither time had anything to do with a hookup or booty call.

But I hadn't explained the first call to Leilani. Had I told her, she might not have reacted the way she did when she saw her calling this time. While the way she reacted was conclusory as hell, I wasn't any better with what I'd said.

It was disrespectful and out of line. More than that, I didn't even feel that way. I just thought of the most hurtful things I could and let that shit spew out of my mouth unfiltered. It was ignorant as hell. Then, to top it off, I blurted out that I loved her. How could she even begin to believe me after the fucked-up shit I said?

It had been a month and no matter what I did, Leilani didn't respond. I sent texts, left voicemails, emailed, and even knocked on the door. I was almost tempted to go to her job with a boombox and flowers in hand—real rom-com style—but I wasn't that desperate or corny.

It would cause her additional strife and not help the situation at all. Especially since I told her some messed up stuff about her job situation. Plus, who did that? This wasn't a movie, a TV show, or some lovey-dovey book. This was real life. I had to talk to her. It was the only way to move forward.

Unfortunately, I knew it wouldn't be any time soon, especially with Cantrell and Midnight having planned some type of surprise birthday thing for me. I sat in my living room waiting for those assholes to come to pick me up. When my phone rang with Leilani's ringtone, I lunged for it. It wasn't her, though. It was Cantrell.

"What?" I muttered.

"Damn, why you mad?" Cantrell chuckled. I heard a car door slam. It wasn't just through the phone though.

"Where are we going?" I walked over to the door, then remembered Midnight had a key. I took my spot on the couch again.

"Oh, I get it. The ringtone pissed you off," Cantrell said.

"Where the fuck are we going, Trell?"

A key engaged the front door before it swung open.

"Nowhere," Cantrell said. "Just going to sit here, get drunk, watch a movie and eat take out from the Chinese spot on Da Block."

I ended the call when they walked inside. Midnight sat a bag of food on the coffee table and stood idly beside the couch. Cantrell sat a second bag down. It probably contained the liquor since I heard glass clink and aluminum shift.

"Happy birthday, asshole." Cantrell clapped me on my back after yanking me to my feet.

"Yeah, thanks," I muttered, only half-ass hugging him in return. "Why the hell did you change my ringtone?"

"You were moping around and talking about Leilani for two weeks straight," he said. "I got sick of it."

"So, changing his ringtone did what exactly?" Midnight asked.

"Nothing, but I wished I could've seen his face," Cantrell said.

"I should kick you in the throat." I squinted my eyes. He shrugged and walked off toward the kitchen.

I hugged Midnight and he squeezed me for a moment. "Happy birthday, bruh."

"Thank you, dude." I let him hold on to me a beat longer. "How are you doing?"

Finally, he pulled back. When he plopped into his seat, I could tell how he might've felt. Much worse than I did. He shook his head. "I can't believe she's gone." He covered his eyes with his palms. I rubbed his back.

"I'm sorry dude. Seriously. It was a lovely service though. Everyone showed such respect to her memory."

"Yeah. It's just shitty as fuck. I miss her like crazy and I don't know what the hell to do anymore."

"With what?"

"Life," Midnight huffed a breath. "She left me the bakery and her house. I had no plans to stay here. You know that. Cantrell knows that. It's just… fuck man."

"I get it. You've been trying to run away from here like there was some type of plague. Why don't you sell the place? You can put it on the market if you want."

Cantrell came back in with a few plates and glasses. "Look, I didn't think the last two weeks were going to go down how they did." He sat the dishes on the table and took a seat opposite Midnight. "I know I've been an annoying ass, but I was just attempting to keep the mood light."

"It's kinda hard to do that when my mother is fucking dead," Midnight managed through gritted teeth. "I had to bury her, man. Bury my mama."

I rubbed a few more circles on his back, but he didn't even move to acknowledge either of our presence for a few more minutes. When it came to friends, these guys had been there since the day we met. There weren't other people on the planet I was closer to besides my sister and her people.

The problem was none of them were talking to me about anything related to Leilani. When everything went down, I got scolded by Missouri. Justice and Chance called and fussed as well.

I had no clue how they were acting with Leilani, or what she'd said, but I didn't explain because they didn't seem to know we'd slept together. I would respect the privacy Leilani seemed to want, but it appeared the others were annoyed with both of us, and not just me.

I sighed and leaned back on the couch, crossing my arms, and looked at the ceiling.

"I'm seriously sorry about your mom, Wolfe," Cantrell said.

"Yeah. I know, dawg. I'm being suss right now." Midnight scrubbed his hand across his face before rising to an upright position. "My bad. Let's eat."

"This is one helluva birthday." I shook my head but didn't move.

Cantrell grabbed up the remote and went about finding a movie for us to watch. Midnight started opening up containers.

"I had big plans for you, dude. Everything changed because it wasn't the time to celebrate like that," Cantrell said. "I'm not about to let you mope all day though. We gon' watch this action-thriller, then we gon' shoot some shit on the game system while we're drunk. Deal?"

"Deal," I sighed.

"That goes for you too, Wolfe," Cantrell added.

"Yeah. I'm doing my best." Midnight spoke around a mouthful of kung pao chicken.

"That's all I can ask for," Cantrell said. "Just put one foot in front of the other."

After we ate and drank nearly all of the beer, we started in on the video games. I didn't feel a lot better, but I could manage to make it through the rest of the night. Work was going smoothly. Construction was underway. Transitions were solid.

I couldn't complain anywhere else in life right now. The real thing that was bugging me was the situation with Leilani and the fact that I had to navigate that while helping my friend through a difficult ass time.

The world didn't revolve around me. I knew I could be a dickwad, but not when it came to situations like this. It might've been my birthday, but I was going to do everything I could to keep my friend in high spirits. I could wait to focus on myself until later.

📖

I woke up with a massive headache, partly because my loud ass ringtone blared in my ear. I grabbed the noise box and silenced it as I rubbed the sleep from my eyes.

When I was finally able to see clearly, I found a reminder email about the dresses and tuxedos. That wasn't the reason for the damn near deafening sound though. I'd received a text from the one person I hoped would reach out.

Leilani: Don't worry about showing up to the dress fittings. It'll be taken care of. As far as the tuxedos go, you can handle that.

Me: Okay. Thank you. Can we talk?

Like every other text I'd sent her, it went unanswered. Lying in bed, I let my mind wander to the times we'd spent together over the past couple of months. It was the most I'd been able to truly see of her since I met her forever ago.

A knock sounded on my door before it pushed open.

"Yo, I'm about to head out," Cantrell's head appeared around the side of the door. "Gotta take Midnight to Sugar Crystal and get in contact with a few people for some work on your San Diego spot."

"Yeah, alright. Good looking."

He gave me a tight-lipped smile.

"Before you leave, how's Wolfe doing?"

Cantrell tilted his head and lifted his lips against his cheek. "Like he said last night, he's trying. We'll have to keep an eye on him."

"Bet."

"This thing with Leilani." I gave him a warning look, but he shook his head and continued. "We've been the three amigos. Three Musketeers. Three blind mice. Whatever you want to call us, we've been tight as hell for a while," he said. "So, I can say this with confidence. If you love that girl as much as it looks like you do, the consistent pushing and prodding is only going to make it worse. I've heard Rumor a plenty of times in the past say that dudes that do too much are the reason why most women don't talk to them again. Give her some space and let her figure out what she wants."

"But—"

"No buts, Alex. Something happened between y'all and you don't want to talk about it. Even with all the stuff that's been swirling on Da Block, you kept your mouth shut," Cantrell said. "That's fine, but unless you decide to open up so we know, you gotta do what she's asking and leave her be. No one knows what the full issue is with y'all. Neither of you seems to want to let anyone in."

"What you mean neither of us?" I sat up. "You've talked to her?"

"I ran into her at the bakery the other day. She asked for a way to reach out to Rumor."

"What in the actual fuck?"

"I don't know, but we'll talk some more later. Let me get Midnight to Sugar Crystal."

"Yeah, alright. Tell him I'll stop by later."

"Bet."

CHAPTER TWENTY-FIVE

ALEXANDER

SPRING GAVE WAY TO SUMMER, and I was left feeling like a complete and utter fool even more. I'd found the cancellation email in my spam. I must've accidentally answered a request sent by Shadow's Peak while I was in and out of consciousness that weekend of catching the flu.

Thinking back to it, I had to have mixed it up with the request to move forward with lighting provided by another vendor that the venue regularly used. I'd meant to cancel that because the quote was outrageous.

I sent Leilani a message letting her know what the mix-up had been, then I left her alone. My friends continued to remind me how impulsive, ignorant and reckless I had been. But at least I had followed Cantrell's advice.

It had been more time than I thought and she still hadn't reached out again. I didn't know what to do at this point. She was my Roni. My mom and dad used to play a lot of old-school music and I remembered the song by Bobby Brown. It was definitely how I felt about her. I realized I was being ignorant and defensive. I had been thinking about so many things over the past few months.

Justice had a different mom, one who was a fully-faceted asshole. She left Dad to raise Justice on his own, and when he started dating my mother, she had the nerve to pretend to care about my sister. That only made it harder for Justice when that woman decided to entirely leave the picture. I didn't think Justice ever really got over it, but I knew the parents she grew to love treated her better than she'd ever have gotten from the other woman. She was an only child for seven years and then I was born, but they didn't make her feel left out.

They still treated her great. I mean she got everything she wanted. Late curfew, big allowance, never got in trouble when she did something wrong. It made me jealous because it felt like I had the leftovers; the smaller allowance, an earlier curfew and I got in trouble for everything.

It took years to understand that there was an age variance, so things were going to be different. But what took me by surprise was when she brought home this really pretty girl. She was nineteen at the time and the chick was quiet and nice.

I felt like she was a gift for me to unwrap. She would be the best friend I could ever ask for. Justice was great, but this girl seemed better. Yet, she didn't pay me any mind. That was upsetting, so I set out to get her to talk to me. I pulled all types of pranks for years. The only time she ever paid attention to me was when she was yelling or complaining.

I was okay with that until one day when I was fifteen, she came over for the Fourth of July and she looked amazing. I was stunned, but my body reacted a different way. It wanted to touch her. My mouth went dry and my dick got hard. I wanted her, wanted to know what it felt like to sink into her like I saw guys do on the porn I secretly watched to get off, but she was twenty-two.

I would never have her in my arms, never know what it

felt like to kiss her and put my hands all over her. So, I continued to prank her for a few more years. By the time I was eighteen, I convinced myself she would never give me the time of day, so I started dating.

I was with a girl for anywhere from a few weeks to a few months. Anything to try to take my mind off the beautiful Leilani, who would never give a guy my age the time of day. After a few years of doing that, I realized I would have to show her how great a person I was.

The night she drove me home because everyone else was too drunk to do so, I never expected to have her in my bed. I felt like there was more to it than the fact that she continuously said we were both in a vulnerable place.

I had already been susceptible to her for years by that point, so if anyone was emotional it was her. I knew that weekend was hard for her because Mother's Day had been coming up and she missed hers. That was why I focused on pleasing her in the best way I knew how. When she left afterward, I knew regret well enough.

Trying to talk to her at my graduation the next day didn't work either. If she were lighter, she would've been red in my presence. She didn't attend my party because she had a work event, but I felt like she would've made an excuse regardless. Since no one seemed to know what happened, I didn't say anything. I also hadn't seen her for years after that.

Leilani managed never to be around when I was. It felt shitty, but I had work and other things to drown myself in. When my sister sprung this wedding stuff on me, I wanted to be mad because I'd been acting like I didn't have feelings for her best friend.

Knowing that I would have to spend six months with her when I knew how much she despised me, had felt like torture and a blessing wrapped up in one bundle. Justice and Chance were convinced I'd be a good change for Leilani and told me

I would have to tell her how I felt. But everything fell apart because of my big damn mouth.

Much of my time was spent at one of the nightclubs overseeing the changes Cantrell and the adjustments to the design Demontré, the interior decorator, was doing for me. I thought about looking for a fifth location but decided to put that off until these four were up and running smoothly after the new look.

When I wasn't nose-deep in work, I spent time with Midnight at Sugar Crystal because he was still trying to figure out his life and what he'd be doing moving forward. Taking over the bakery full-time wasn't something he wanted to do but he couldn't see parting ways with it just yet either.

"Why are you sitting up here by yourself with a whole ass party happening down there?" Justice's voice pulled me out of my scramble of thoughts. I looked up in time to see her closing my office door behind her. She glowered at me, but I wasn't in the mood.

"I've got work to do."

"What work? You've been staring at your computer, eyes not moving and hands in your lap." *How long had she stood in my doorway to know that?* She walked over to the couch across from my desk and took a seat. "No, 'hey sister, so glad to know you made it back safely?'"

"I'm glad you're okay and I hope you had fun on tour. Why are you here?"

"I came to see what the hell happened between you and Leilani because she won't talk about it," Justice said. "And I'm sick of her dragging ass around the apartment."

I perked up. "She's what?"

"She's upset and it has to be with you since the two of you haven't worked on shit together in at least three months."

I rolled my eyes and flopped back in my chair.

"I thought as much." Justice readjusted her ponytail and toed off her slip-ons. "Since she isn't telling me what happened. I'm going to make an educated guess because if she pops off on me one more time—"

"Why she at your neck?"

"Well, the one thing she did share was that you were a complete imbecile," Justice said. "She had to work all of the rest of the planning by herself. I might've let it slip that pairing you too was a mistake but I thought it would be good for both of you."

"Justice, you're a bit ignorant for that."

The expression on her face told me I was a second away from losing my life.

"No, let me tell you who's ignorant. You. I helped set up the perfect way to spend time with her," she said. "What do you do? Fuck it up. I know it was more than the venue snafu, which by the way, thanks. I really wanted that spot."

"Was she able to get it back? I'm sorry. I really am. Since no one is talking to me and all I'm getting is a bunch of emails and shit, I don't check them as often."

"No, she's still working on it. But seriously bro… what happened with y'all?"

"If she didn't tell you, it's not my place to say."

"She's behaving the same way she did right after your graduation, except this time she's angrier and I swear I heard her cry."

"She cried?" My face scrunched. I closed my eyes and tilted my head away from my sister. I didn't want Leilani in tears because of me. *Fuck.* I heard Justice rise to her feet. When her hand lifted my head toward her, I opened my eyes.

"Did you guys have sex?"

I didn't respond. Instead, I averted my gaze.

"Okay, that makes a lot more sense. This must've been the second time because of the similarities in her behavior."

Justice leaned her head back in a silent laugh. "Why didn't you tell me?"

It wasn't the second time, nor the third or fourth, but she didn't need those details.

"I'm grown, Justice. Why would I tell my sister about who I was sleeping with?"

"Because I knew you had feelings for her and she doesn't do relationships. I never even saw her with a man, to be honest," she said. "I teased her about still being a virgin, but I knew she wasn't. But like, the two of y'all? If you guys had sex, that would explain so much of the past four years."

"Huh? What are you talking about?"

"Nothing. Listen, I'll talk to her." She rubbed her hand across her face. "I love you, and I have to remember you are younger than us. No matter how deep my love is, you're also still a guy. That means doing or saying something foolish all the damn time."

"Let me tell you what happened."

"Okay." She grabbed my hand and walked us over to the couch. "Shoot."

I laid out everything that happened from the day we went to Oceanside up until me being a doofus with her in this very room a few weeks before my birthday. Justice hopped to her feet and went to sit on the corner of my desk. I cocked my head.

"What are you doing?" I asked.

"You fucked my friend on that couch. How dare you not say something before I put my bare thighs on it?"

I couldn't help but laugh. A genuine one for the first time in months. "It's been cleaned, weirdo."

"Whatever. Next time, warn me."

"Okay. If there's a next time, I'll let you know."

"Now that I know what went down, I can talk to her. She's going to be pissed you told me about y'all sleeping together and all the flirty and relationship shit in between, but I'll deal with that. How's about not blowing shit out of proportion next time?"

"Defensive and apprehensive is my default when I feel attacked. Sorry. I've been working on it," I said. "Rumor has always been and will always be the one for Cantrell, even though they want to remain blind to it."

"Yeah, okay. Whatever. Let me go see what I can do. Just keep up the good work around the clubs. I got you." Justice walked over to me. I rose to my feet and pulled her into a back-breaking hug.

"Sorry if I caused a rift between you and your friend. I'll do better. I love you, sister."

"No rift. She's just been really tense and wouldn't talk about it. She and Missouri weren't even really speaking either. It was uncomfortable is all," she said. "But I love you too, brother. Now stop being an ass and I'll see you soon. Okay?"

"Alright."

The following day, Colin popped his head into my office.

"Hey boss, I've been informed to let you know that the Hidden Cravings drink you and Leilani selected has been added to the menu," he said. "I'll be handling the bachelorette party and the wedding festivities, so I put the time off request in just as a reminder."

"No worries. Thank you for volunteering for it and reminding me of the request. You let—"

"Your big-headed ass club manager is aware and she approved it. Everything is set to go."

I laughed. Him and Freddie had butted heads for the longest. I was thankful he mostly answered to Barkley except for time requests because those two could get annoying at times.

"Solid. Thanks, Colin."

He nodded and went on his way. Leilani was in no way trying to speak to me if she went directly to my bartender. I already knew she was avoiding me, but damn. Everything might be ready for the wedding, except the woman I wanted knowing how much I loved her.

Leilani was not ready for me. I wasn't sure if she ever would be, and that niggling fact scared me. Even if she didn't realize it, I'd gotten her to come out of her shell more than I'd ever seen before.

She'd gone on a nice long drive down the coast with me. She stayed in a room with me, even though she could have asked to be in the main house with her best friend's family.

Leilani walked around a wedding venue with me, even though I screwed up in the end. There were many other things she did including flirting, kissing me, and having sex, even though that too I fucked up.

While her outfits may have been simple over those couple of months we'd spent together, she'd dressed sexier. She wore things that showed off her figure and her legs a bit more. Leilani had almost always kept covered because most of her less pigmented skin was on her lower extremities.

The most important thing that let me know she'd stepped out of her comfort zone was when she invited me into her bed, sick or not. That wasn't something I ever imagined her doing.

I hoped Justice could find a way to convince Leilani that my age wasn't a factor, and that while I'd been a complete ignoramus, I wanted to be hers.

CHAPTER TWENTY-SIX

LEILANI

"You're taking two weeks off, right?" One of the members of my team asked.

"Yeah, last-minute wedding stuff. I'll have everything ready for you guys for that book launch, though," I said. "I'll also be on standby, but don't be calling and annoying me over nothing."

The woman walked off laughing. I looked around my office knowing I'd be leaving this place soon. It was an amazing beginning and held memories I'd never forget. I'd been able to do great things with this publisher.

It was where I'd gotten my start, but between wanting to hide away, all of the wedding stuff and what Alexander had me thinking about over the past couple of months, I finally knew event planning was where I wanted to be.

Alexander might've said things that were messed up, and I should've knocked his ass out for it, but he hadn't been wrong. I was happier hiding away and listening to other people tell me what to do even though I was more talented than the position I held. I had to build myself up before I could go back and tell him how right he'd been.

Beyond the fact that my feelings hadn't subsided even though I'd kept my distance and he'd left me alone as I wanted, I needed to show him and myself that I could be more than I was letting on.

I'd even taken time to jot down what I remembered from the conversations we'd had about how he wanted to branch out his clubs and brand them in a new light. I wrote marketing plans and ideas down that might be beneficial if he decided to use them. All that didn't even happen until after I'd spoken to Rumor, though.

She was very nice. We talked about how she'd met Alex and how much she wanted to bop him upside his head for never telling me how they knew each other. She even told me about how he'd been simping since the day they'd met.

Alexander had never even as much as glanced her way. I felt foolish for losing faith in him after I'd seen him do exactly what he'd done in the dress shop. His attention was glued to me, he'd assured me there was nothing there, but I was hoping for an out and took her call as my way to run before it got too serious.

My brain and my mouth weren't on the same page no matter how much I thought they were. I apologized to her for how cold I'd been when we met. She said he was the one at fault for not explaining everything. But that wasn't true. I had jumped to conclusions.

Rumor even told me about the two phone calls that I'd been bothered by. The first night had been about Cantrell and the second about Midnight.

I felt terrible about overreacting, but ultimately Alex's comments were the problem. It didn't have to go that far—that was why I had refused to deal with him.

As I finished reading over the itinerary and the full lineup for the book event that my team would handle while I was away for the wedding, I received a text from my new friend.

. . .

Rumor: *Hey, Leilani. I still think this new line I'm making would look great in your undies drawer.*

She attached a photo of a lingerie set that was absolutely to die for, but I'd never see myself in it. I smiled and responded with an emoji that hid my face and said it wasn't going to happen. I might've been freer in mind to show skin and be out there, but that bedroom fit was something else. I wasn't quite to that point.

Even with the bachelorette party tonight, I'd be cute but not too much. The main thing I needed to do was wrap my head around seeing Alexander. I'd finally found the words I wanted to say.

When Justice confronted me about sleeping with Alexander, I wanted to kill him for telling her, but it made it so much easier. I hadn't been sure how she'd react. I knew she'd been teasing and prodding, but it actually happening? When she said the past four years made sense, I couldn't believe there had been a tell. But it was nice to have it off my chest.

I'd shared my side of the story with her and Missouri, filling in the blanks Alexander left out or didn't know. Chance found out everything later. She said she'd kick his ass if I wanted her to, but I didn't. *Ha. Wow. I really didn't.*

They'd told me to take whatever time I needed, which ended up being a surplus of more than a month. Mainly so I could apologize for my reaction and cutting him off how I had.

They almost thought not being around him would make me happier, and for a while, I did too. I'd felt bad for hiding it from them, but knowing they had my back regardless made it all the better.

After finishing at the office, I went home and prepared to go out for a night of delight with my friends and the rest of the bridal party. I wasn't used to this more skin thing quite yet, but I waltzed into the living room exuding confidence anyway.

My hair had been pinned up in what I could only imagine looked like some fluffy flower, except my bangs were out. Letting them cut even two inches of my hair scared me to death, but I was trying new things thanks to a more accepting and freer version of myself, one I could give Alexander credit for.

Even then, I still didn't look at my reflection. Some things should be left as a surprise. I knew I was wearing a fire engine red dress that was tight and short and shimmered in the light like a thousand diamonds. It was definitely different for me, but everything from now until the wedding day was for Justice.

"Well, don't you look stunning?" Tristan said. The girls all turned around.

"*Damn, Gina,*" Justice said.

I laughed. Chance just shook her head in disbelief. "Is that really you? Check out the beauty you've been hiding from us all this time."

"Oh, hush." I adjusted my foot in my ankle booties with the thin stiletto heel.

"Nah, sister guh. You've been hiding that body under those floppy clothes. I knew you were beautiful but damn." Missouri came over, then pulled me toward the door. Someone grabbed my purse before we departed.

"Come on, come on, come on. We have to go." Justice was too excited. "The bus will be downstairs in like two minutes."

Once we were all on board, I realized Alexander was the

only one missing. It should've been ten of us, but nope. I looked around and recounted like five times.

"He's not here," Chance yelled over the music. "He said he didn't want to make things awkward, so he would skip it."

I was sitting down, drink in hand, which was what made me think of him in the first place. I mean, I wasn't fully prepared to see him, but I knew it would be happening for the next few days. Now I wasn't sure how I felt that he wasn't here tonight.

Sad? Disappointed? Ecstatic? Relieved?

Everything kind of went by in a blur after that. We drank too much, they danced a lot, and we had VIP treatment at probably three bars. I got pretty drunk and didn't remember part of the night.

Which was way out of my norm. By the time we got back to the apartment, I was pretty sure we were holding Justice and Chance up. Honestly, we were probably holding each other up. It was all laughs and lots of sloshed walking.

The heels came off the moment we stepped off the elevator on our floor. We were done with almost breaking our ankles and necks and everything in between. It was the countdown to the wedding now, just six days to go.

The week was filled with last-minute work for everyone. Well, almost everyone. The happy couple had to get things in before they were off on their after-wedding adventures. Renee Lanai was sad she was going to be missing her assistant but was happy Justice was getting married. The singer paid for their honeymoon, which included a tour of Europe that would probably be super extravagant.

Moves paid for half of the wedding. Their top spokesperson was getting married and that meant big things for them as well. Chance thought it was funny, but she didn't complain—that was why they'd been able to let us go all out on most of the aspects and elements of the wedding. The organization wanted a special edition shoot after the honeymoon. It was all looking up for the two brides.

Chance owned a house, which made Missouri realize Justice would probably move in with her soon after they returned from their trip. She mentioned that we should probably downsize to a three-bedroom because we wouldn't need two extra rooms. We decided to wait to discuss it in detail until after they got back.

With Zuri slightly less busy than she'd been over the past few months, we would figure out our new life without our third girl constantly around. It wasn't like either of us would be any less busy, except me especially if I quit my job and started anew, but we'd always find a way to hang out and do stuff.

📖

A COUPLE of days before the wedding, I woke up thinking about what Mercedes and my dad had said a few months ago. I also thought back to the conversation I'd had with Justice, Chance, and Missouri. I focused on how happy everyone was. It brought a smile to my face, and, for the first time in months, I wished I had those things as well.

I regretted waiting until after thirty to even think about it, but ultimately what occupied my mind as I laid in bed was the man who'd practically ripped my heart out and stomped on it before shoving it back down my throat. Even though he was nothing more than my friend's annoying younger brother that I had sex with, and had fallen in love with.

I knew I needed to speak to Alexander and the time for that to happen was basically upon me. Half the week had blown by. It was the day of the rehearsal dinner, and everything was freaking me out. I'd ignored him for so long,

I knew this would be completely terrible or next-level awkward no matter how we went about it. That ball of twine in Kansas still had nothing on me.

This time I was ten times worse than that, though.

Once we made it to the venue, I huffed as we sat around the table. To my knowledge, Alexander hadn't checked in yet. It was like him to be late to everything, but one would think he could have been on time for the damn rehearsal dinner for his own sister's wedding. Everyone looked around nervously because apparently, I wasn't the only one who hadn't heard from him.

The reverend, whom Chance loved dearly and had asked to officiate, was about to start speaking when Alex barreled into the room and took his seat opposite me. We were sitting around the rectangular table in the order of how we would enter for the event. At a second table sat Chance and Justice's closest family members, who weren't bridesmen or bridesmaids, but were important to the ladies.

"Sorry I'm late. I got down here a few hours ago and thought I could manage a couple of hours' sleep. That was a bad idea," Alexander said. "I'm sorry sis. I'm sorry Chance."

I scoffed quietly, but he'd heard me, and so did Missouri and the brides-to-be. I was pretty sure even the reverend heard. If anyone else in the room had, they didn't react.

"My bad," I whispered.

The reverend began going over how everything would proceed and what each of us would need to do. Once he finished his instructions, we practiced our entrances, the setup for the ceremony, and how the entire event would proceed.

Plus, we went over seating for the reception. Some of that didn't need to be discussed but Chance and Justice wanted to just because. They'd asked to see the setup, but I told them they'd have to wait until the day of.

The last thing we did was one final rehearsal of our dance routines. Each side did theirs without interference. It was a jam-packed afternoon, but everyone was very excited for the dinner portion of the night. Since I hadn't spoken to Alexander in months, I planned this without him. Missouri helped, and once Chance and Justice were back in town, they were excited to be a part of the planning as well.

Once we were seated for dinner, the conversations started up in record time. I sat quietly. I was enjoying my salad and wine while waiting on my baked ziti. Justice thought it was perfect to have that and a few other options since I'd done everything to make her big day amazing. I was in my zone until Missouri nudged me.

"What?" I said absentmindedly.

"Answer the question." She looked toward Chance.

I followed her gaze, confusion written all over my face.

Chance chuckled.

"I asked when it would be our turn to watch you walk down the aisle. Missouri said her money is on the next two years. She and Tristan are betting you fall head over heels for someone very soon," she said. "We think it might take a little longer. Maybe five years. We think you'll be in the courting stage for quite a while. Then you'll decide if marriage is truly on the table."

I shifted my eyes across everyone's faces. They'd all stopped their conversations and were waiting for me to answer. Everyone had their attention on me except for Alexander who was more into his soup than this topic. *Figures.* It was more than evident they were hinting at him, but I wasn't taking that bait. No matter if they knew what happened between us, I hadn't admitted to loving him.

I cleared my throat and looked back at my salad, stabbing at a mostly empty plate.

"I don't know. Never saw it in my cards. Never thought

about it until recently." I felt Alexander's eyes shift toward me, but I kept mine cast down. "I had a few conversations with a couple of people. They made me realize that I was hiding from commitment, but I had already fully committed to a few people. Justice, Missouri, Tristan, Chance. I mean, Christopher has known me the longest. I have his wife Mercedes and their children. I have my dad. And most annoying of all I have Alex."

I looked up and his eyes locked on mine. We stayed that way for a few seconds.

"I don't know when I'll walk down the aisle, or if I ever will. What I do know is that I'll give myself a shot at what my parents once had, what Chris has. What Missouri is building and what Justice and Chance are about to seal," I said. "A chance at a family and a long-lasting love. For now, I'm just lil' ol' me."

Everyone was silent for a moment before applause filled the room. I looked around and shook my head. They were a mess. Every single last one of them. I almost laughed, but what took me by surprise and stopped me from doing just that was Alexander walking around the table to kneel in front of me.

He had to be kidding. This was some kind of sick joke. Everyone got quiet and moved into a better position so they could see what was happening. Justice and Chance were not doing well hiding their giddiness. They knew something. I swiveled in my chair so I could face him.

"What are you doing?" I asked.

"Something that I've been wanting to do for a long time." Alexander pulled a small box from his pocket and everyone gasped. I lowered one eyebrow, while the other one raised. Was he really being serious right now?

I wiped my forehead and rested my hand over my mouth, leaning it on my thigh. Making sure to keep my legs pressed together, otherwise, he would get a full show. He smiled, looking me dead in my eyes. It was as if he read my body language and my mind.

"Will you—" Alexander started and then began opening the box. "Will you wear these on an official, non-negotiated, non-obligatory date with me?"

The box popped open to reveal a pair of beautiful aquamarine studded earrings. They were gorgeous, but I about slapped him.

I had a lopsided grin and my lips poked out in shock. I could really punch him right now. I really could. I shook my head and his sexy little smirk appeared.

"So? Will you?" I heard snickering from behind me.

"Sure, kid. Why not?" I smiled. "Everyone deserves a shot at love, right?"

That was what my dad would've said. So, I guessed that included my friend's kid brother. Now to get past this wedding and see what the future held for me and the brat.

CHAPTER TWENTY-SEVEN

ALEXANDER

I COULDN'T BEGIN to tell you how Leilani pulled it off, but everything looked amazing. This morning, she'd knocked on my door and barged in as soon as I opened it.

"How are you not dressed already?" she asked. "Do you expect me to do this all on my own? Still?"

I yawned and stared at her as I worked to see her straight. She wore cut-off shorts and an off-the-shoulder near-sheer top. I thought I was dreaming until she pulled me toward the bathroom and told me I had five minutes to clean up so we could make sure everything was coming together as it should.

Up until 11 a.m., we were checking in with every different person on the beach making sure everything from the way the flowers were laid on the sand to the positioning of the centerpieces was correct. The cake had to be stored off-site. We went to check on it. She'd finalized the design and colors, so I didn't know what it looked like until Chef Amanda showed us. It was incredible.

At noon, Leilani started freaking out. "What do you mean? You'll be back? How the hell could you take an assignment the afternoon before your best friend's wedding, Zuri?"

Leilani's focus zeroed in on me as she paced back and forth across the sand outside of the tent.

"I understand it was supposed to be quick or whatever, but your flight back was supposed to arrive an hour ago," she said. "The next one has a weird ass layover. There's no way you'll get here on time. Now you have to drive. You need to leave like now. What were you thinking?"

There was a pause. "Fine, well tell that football player that I couldn't care less about his last-minute 'thing,'" she said. "If he doesn't get you here on time and bring a fucking gift for the inconvenience and headache, I'm going to kick him in his kneecaps. I'd like to see him go up and down the field then."

I grimaced and was glad Leilani had never threatened me, but could only imagine what she'd thought over the past few months. After she finally hung up, I pulled her to the side.

"I know you agreed to go on a real date, not a dare-style thing with me, but I still wanted to apologize for what I sa—"

Leilani put her finger to my lips before removing it and kissing me. It wasn't a peck either. She gripped the back of my neck and kept me in place. I found my hands going to her nape and the small of her back as the moment progressed. A throat clearing was the only reason we stopped.

The florist had a question about the way some of the flowers were supposed to hang in the tent since the wind was making a bit of a problem for her. Leilani smiled as she wiped the corner of my mouth.

"I have something to say, but I'll tell you after I handle this," she said. "Go make sure the ceremony set up isn't being tossed around because of this wind, will you?"

Some of the flowers had blown away, but it actually made the area look homier and more romantic. Securing the columns near the seating area and the archway Justice and

Chance were to stand in front of was already underway when I walked over. I checked in with the men and women who were handling it. They assured me that once they had the anchors in place, everything would be fine.

"This looks amazing, doesn't it?" Leilani came to a stop beside me.

She seemed to be taking in the beauty of the ocean at our side and the scene she'd brought to life. While she admired that, I couldn't help but look at her.

"Quite stunning, I'd say."

Leilani turned her head toward me before smiling.

"I should have chopped your balls off and fed them to a wild animal after the things you said to me that night. I was angry for a long time," she said. "A. Long. Time. Then I took a moment to think about it and you were right. I was scared to step out of myself, out of my job, my everything."

She took a deep breath.

"I'm planning on quitting and starting my own event planning business, or maybe even starting up my own freelance public relations thing. It was something I'd thought about while still in college." Leilani waved a hand down her side. "As you can see, I'm not hiding my body as much as I used to, but I'm still getting used to showing this much. The most important thing I think you said that night… What might've bothered me the most was that everything happened because we were stuck together on this. That's partially true."

I couldn't believe how proud I was of this woman, this woman who seemed to care about me, for opening up to me like this. It took a lot for her, and it made me love her a little bit more.

Leilani grabbed my hand and walked me back toward the tent. "It wasn't really the being stuck with you that made me act as I had, but more so the freedom I felt from my overlapping thoughts. You're one of my best friend's siblings and you're younger than me," she said. "I thought something had to be wrong because how could I like some kid I'd met when he was basically just out of elementary? I felt weird for even thinking of you as a fully-fledged adult. I ignored the fact that…"

Her eyes ran the length of my body and it made me a little self-conscious.

"Well, that you are nowhere near a kid anymore. All the pranks and impulsive shit was in the past. Yeah, you can be arrogant and narrow-minded, but you are smart and know how to do things," she said. "You run multiple businesses, damn well I might add. You took care of me and got yourself sick when you could've just left me to fend for myself."

She stopped for a moment, turning toward me and holding both of my hands in hers. "You tolerated all of my assumptions and overall asshole-ishness when you didn't have to. Plus, after I'd treated you like a one-night stand and ignored you for almost four years, you still tried to speak to me whenever you came around," she said. "And you agreed to do this for your sister, knowing I was involved and probably wouldn't want to be bothered with you. If anybody owes anybody an apology, I think it's me. So, I wanted to tell you this before, but—"

I yanked her against me, eliciting the gasp I'd hoped.

"No matter how you try to swing it…" I pushed her kinky hair out of her face. "I was a dick for what I said and how I acted. We were having sex, Leilani. I told you not to worry about the girl calling my phone in the middle of the night. I never explained who she was to me," I said. "Then I named everything about you that you were insecure about. I was pretty sure, if not for this wedding, I'd never have heard from you again. I promise that I'll never say or do something hurtful like that ever again. Next time I'm inside you, not only will I be the only thing preoccupying your mind, I'll get you to come for me multiple times, again."

I kissed Leilani before she could respond and it was like sealing the deal and making a promise. This wasn't the end nor a trial situation, this was our beginning.

She pulled back, smiling.

"First, never stop telling me what you want to do to me." Leilani nipped my lower lip. "It catches me off guard and it makes me forget myself. You remember that comment in the restaurant? I half wanted you to climb your ass under that table and do it."

"I can recreate the moment if you like." I captured her lips once more.

They intoxicated me. Being able to kiss her again was like being granted a second life. She broke the embrace and stepped away, sucking in a deep breath.

"You're making it difficult for me to remember what I wanted to tell you," she said, then snapped. "Okay, right. Second, I wanted to tell you I'm sorry. Like actually sorry. I'd thought about how I could show you for a long time. I ended up creating marketing plans to help grow your clubs even more. It was the only way I could think to apologize for blowing up on you."

I shook my head and brought her back into my arms. "All that doesn't matter," I said. "I appreciate it, but you being right here is the only thing that will make me smile until the day I cease to exist."

"I love you, Alexander Rutherford. I might have wanted to wring your neck years ago, shit a few months ago too, but I love you with every ounce of my being," Leilani said. "I have a question though."

I leaned forward and kissed her again. I had a feeling I knew what she was going to ask. She dug her fingers into the curls that had started to sprout from my scalp, tugging just enough for me to pull back. I smiled against her lips before moving so I could see her eyes.

"Quit it with the distractions that mouth can do." Leilani grinned. "The earrings. What made you buy those if I hadn't spoken to you in months? They're beautiful, but…"

"Might've had spies feeding me intel," I said. "People had seen a shift in your mood and told me, but more than that. It was a crystal that looked like the ocean and had properties that were supposed to help with emotional trauma."

I rubbed my thumb along her cheek. "Even if you never spoke to me again, I wanted to do something that could help heal you of my ignorance and the pain I knew you still felt when it came to your mother."

Leilani's eyes grew wide. "What are you talking about?"

"I knew you slept with me that first time because you were hoping for a distraction," I said. "Mother's Day weekend. I hoped it was more than that, but I'd known this whole time."

"Why didn't you say anything?"

"Because, if I could help, that was more important," I said. "I have loved you for so long. I've only ever wanted you. I've only wanted to see you happy. I've only ever desired to have you with me. I've wanted to be the man in your story that brought you joy for the rest of your days."

"This isn't a romance novel, Alex." She hugged herself closer to me. "It's real life. I can say you've behaved like a hardheaded love interest though, and now you're mine. Our story doesn't end like they do in the books, it's continuing after this chapter ends."

My smile grew and my eyes melted closed. I felt her shift in my arms until her lips were on mine again.

M ISSOURI MADE it for the ceremony and even got ready and cussed out with plenty of time left over. The bridesmaids looked amazing in their full-length mauveine dresses. Justice's gown had hints of the color scattered through the sparkling sequin part of her train. She looked amazing. The bridesmen wore white suits with ties and pocket squares that matched the women and Chance's dress which hugged her every curve.

It was sheer everywhere besides the lace cutouts that covered her essentials and the bottom of the outfit. I only knew what any of these elements were because the designer had gone over everything ad nauseam when we were at the shop that day. Then when I went to the tux fitting, the women assisting us made sure we knew how our suits were complementing the dresses and the brides' gowns.

Scanning the crowd as the reverend spoke, I spotted my parents, Chance's aunt and cousin, Leilani's dad, Missouri's aunt, the football player that drove Missouri down, Chris and Mercedes, Rumor, my best friends, and Demontre.

The one person who wasn't out there was Ego, who I hadn't heard from since she agreed to come back to the area to sing and dance at Haze. I didn't think she'd given up on it based on the stories still circulating, but I thought she would have made the wedding.

All of that melted away when my attention fell on Leilani. While the gown was long and covered her from the chest down, her arms were on full display and her hair was braided back into a beautiful half-fro. After our conversation earlier, I was finally feeling like things were getting better. I couldn't know for sure what was coming next, but having her by my side was more than I could ever ask for.

I'd missed the vows, but tuned in long enough to present the rings since I had them. I watched as my sister fought back tears and heard the awes and sniffles coming from the audience.

When the reverend announced their union, cheers exploded and Justice and Chance shared their kiss, but my attention remained on Leilani who caught my eye and had a shy smile on her face. She began clapping as the happy couple walked off down the sand.

Soon after the bridal party followed their recession, the two of us jogged over to make sure everything for the reception was ready. We showed the room to Chance and Justice first because Leilani wanted their honest untapped reaction. They loved it. From the multiple tones of purple and pink that colored every surface to the 'Scales of justice taking a chance on love' centerpieces on their table, everything was a hit.

Once everyone had been seated and dinner had been served, speeches started up. Of course, Chance's brother gave one and it had most of the women and a couple of the men in tears.

My dad gave a speech about seeing his little girl happy. It had a similar effect on everyone, including me. Missouri talked about the support and love Justice had shown her, the way she treated her like a sister in the absence of her own— only because of distance—and how happy and excited she was to see this new chapter starting.

"The last thing I have to say is my sister overnighted one of the most delicious looking chocolate mousse cakes I've ever seen. I can't wait for you guys to get back to your suite and find it hiding in your mini-fridge," she said. "She sends her regards and says she wishes she could've been the one to cater for you, but can't wait to see you both again one day soon."

When it got to Leilani, she talked about learning love and the hardships of relationships from watching those around her. She said she knew, in the end, the right things always triumphed. Her saying that let me know what she'd told me earlier was more than real.

Leilani speech had been modified, she said, which let me know she made adjustments after our little encounter at the rehearsal a couple of days ago. When my time came, I was terrified but ready. I'd get to speak about both of these amazing brides because of my position in the bridal party.

I stood and everyone remained silent. "I won't try to bring you to tears or pull on your heartstrings. I also don't have a prepared speech because I just couldn't think of what I wanted to say about these two amazing people. I'll keep it short and sweet, I promise, but until this moment, I was at a loss for words."

I looked around the room, my eyes landing on Leilani for a moment before I turned to look at my sister and her wife.

"I knew love because of our amazing parents, Justice. I knew one day I would want what they had, but I also knew that exact pairing wasn't for you. Your love was out of this world and didn't stop for anybody's ideals." I smiled. "It took you some time to accept that and learn it yourself, but from the moment I met Chance I knew she was the one you'd be with."

My sister squinted her eyes at me but had a smile on her face.

"Chance, you flew into her life and turned her way of thinking upside down. She thought she was ready, but she wasn't. Everything made sense to her until it didn't. She didn't know how to handle it. Neither of you did for a long time."

My eyes drifted to Leilani for a moment. I knew she'd caught on to what I was saying beneath it all. "You gave her the time she needed. When she came back into your life it was the light both of you had sought for so long finally coming on again."

Leilani's intake of breath was evident from here. I returned my attention to the lovely brides who were looking in her direction as well before shifting their attention back to me.

"You both taught me a lot over the years, but nothing more than to say what I mean, love who I love, and fight for what I want," I said. "Things might get hard, but that doesn't mean you should give up. I know your life together will be amazing. I can't wait to see what the future brings. I love you both."

When I returned to my seat beside Leilani, she grabbed my hand beneath the table before leaning over to kiss the corner of my mouth. She'd received my message about us loud and clear. It was a new life for more than one couple, and I was prepared to do whatever it took to see this happy ending unfold every day for the rest of my existence.

THANK YOU

If you enjoyed this book, please consider leaving a review on the website in which you purchased it and/or my Goodreads page. As an indie author, reviews are key to helping the next reader discover a book they may love.

Book two, Uncovering Her Hunger, follows Midnight and Desire.

Also, sign up for my newsletter to keep up-to-date with what I'm working on.

Thank you and I hope you enjoyed it.
    Love,
    Rae Shawn

ACKNOWLEDGMENTS

I have to thank Meka James first and foremost. This series has been revamped and rediscovered. If she hadn't beta-read one of the later books, I wouldn't have gone back and started to rework other aspects of this entire series.

It was a lot of work, but my editor helped me make this book a dream. The Wordmakers were super encouraging and supportive when I wanted to give up and say screw it.

I have to thank Lisa Kessler for asking me to come on her podcast, Book Lights. If she hadn't asked, I probably would've found more and more reasons to push this off, but I didn't want to show up without a new project coming out, so here we are.

My Write Owls, I love y'all dearly. The late nights on Zoom, laughing, stressing, working our asses off, or just chilling after a long day was the best.

D. Ann, KK, Ali, Karmen, and Mia ... y'all weren't playing any games when I was on my bullshit. Thanks for keeping that fire lit under my ass and for telling me to add MORE to this story. More sex, more emotions, more thoughts, just more everything. Y'all asked for it, y'all got it.

Tasha L. Harrison ... ma'am. Once again, you introduced me to this group of amazing people from all over the globe. Thank you for the constant encouragement, and kicks in the ass.

To my Mama, thank you for not feeling like I was ignoring you whenever I got super into focus mode and didn't answer texts.

Most importantly, to my readers, thank you for reading. Your comments and your love are not unnoticed. None of this would work without all of you.

PREVIEW - UNCOVERING HER HUNGER

DESIRE

Drifting through a kitchen always left a smile on my face. The smell of the ingredients for dinner and dessert wafting together, the laughter and banter of the other chefs lifting into the air, the random playlist that blasted from the corner of the room; everything made each day brighter.

The only difference between any other time and today was that I was catering my coworker's engagement party, alongside my best friend. Normally, we'd be working in the private kitchen of one of the most influential couples in Decatur, but we had the night off for Halloween and the fact that our pastry chef was having her event.

Rochelle, the bride-to-be, asked if we could all take the day for her celebration. The couple we all worked for was more than accommodating; they even paid for the rental hall. Me and my best friend, Eliza, planned to just attend and have fun. Instead, we decided to gift a drama-free night with delicious food and a surprise dessert for the person who always made the last dish well worth the wait.

The fun part was getting to see Rochelle prancing about telling everyone how excited she was to finally tie the knot. Here I was, still the single and reckless friend who got down with anybody who wanted to give me the goods. These two chicks were out here, loving up their boos they'd been with for years now, but that was finally changing.

I'd made a vow on my birthday two weeks ago and I'd stuck to it thus far. It was time I found exactly what I wanted instead of the short-term wham, bam, thank you, ma'am. It was time to build a connection with a person instead of having sex just because I wanted to. No more one-night stands.

I took a deep breath and looked around the kitchen. Everyone, including Eliza, was smiling and laughing as they went about prepping the various courses. We'd hired a couple of people to help us get things running smoothly, and perfect couldn't begin to describe how well it had gone thus far.

I slipped out of the kitchen and made my way to the dining area to double-check that the dishware had been set up properly. While on my way to the table in the far corner, I glanced in the direction of the ongoing party, wondering if I'd have time to go meet some of Rochelle and her fiancé's cute single friends.

Stop.

Taking a deep breath, I walked around the room, surveying the tables. Two were missing salad plates and soup spoons, so I needed to grab the dishes. As I turned around, I bumped into someone and something fell out of their hand. Reaching out, I caught the item and turned it over in mine.

"I'm so sorry, I-" Looking up to see a man dressed in all black, with his dreads piled into a haphazard bun atop his head, stole the rest of my sentence.

His mouth twitched before a smile appeared, along with a deep dimple on his cheek. He stretched out his open palm toward me. I shook my head and sat the camera lens I'd caught in his hand.

"Hope I didn't mess up the glass," I muttered.

"I'm sure it's fine," he said. "That's my fault for trying to walk and screw a lens on at the same time."

I watched his throat bob as he spoke. He was fine enough to fuck on principle alone. I had to quickly remind myself I couldn't sleep with this man. Not only did I have work to do, but I'd also made a commitment.

The sleeping around had been to get over the woman who broke my heart, and knowing she was going to get married soon hurt me to my core. It made me feel unworthy and that wouldn't do. I'd find the one for me one day. Wasting a lot of time with anyone – including this fine-ass man standing in front of me – would defeat the purpose of the vow I'd made to myself.

The lick of his lips knotted my stomach and I had to look anywhere else but at him. The things he could probably do with— "I should get back to what I was doing." I started to walk away, but he called out to me.

"I didn't catch your name, or why you were randomly in a dining room that's closed off until dinner," he said. "There aren't supposed to be guests back here."

"You're nosy aren't ya?" I grinned, glancing back at him.

"Only when I'm a little perplexed by a beautiful woman." He raised an eyebrow. "And now I'm wondering what that tattoo peeking out on your hip is."

I glanced down before righting my shirt. "Under different circumstances, I'd…" I returned my gaze to his.

His confidence was one thing, but damn if he wasn't just a beautiful man. That goatee, those eyes, and the way he bit his lip. Damn, I'd fuck him to sleep if I wasn't trying to get my life together.

"You'd what?" He took a step toward me. He'd screwed the lens onto the camera and let it hang from his hip.

"You're the photographer?" I nodded toward the device hugging him like I'd like to.

"Yeah, and you are?"

"The chef. Speaking of, I should get back and check on the food." I smiled and inclined my head, before turning and walking off.

"I'll see you around then," he called. I waved my hand at him over my shoulder.

There was absolutely no way I'd be seeing him again because if I did, things would happen and none of them would be good, bad, or forgettable. When I walked back into the kitchen my best friend pulled me to the side.

"What in the fresh hell are you doing?" Eliza asked.

"Coming back in here to help plate the food and check on the main course." I looked at her, slight confusion lacing my features.

"You know damn well what I'm talking about." She pushed the door open just enough so I could see the photographer snapping photos of the setup.

"Cute, ain't he?" I grinned.

"Desire, we talked about this. You've had nearly two weeks of not trying to bed a rando." She pulled me away from the door. "You bump into this sexy beast of a man and you're ready to yank his clothes off? Don't break your word already. Your ex damn near ran you into the ground, but you said no more of the good good until—"

"I'm sticking to my guns." I stood a little straighter. She only ever used my full name when she was making a point or joking and wanted it to be clear. "I damn sure thought about messing with him, but I'm not going to. I literally went to check and make sure everything was good in there. He bumped into me."

Eliza leveled me with a look.

"I made a promise to myself," I said. "It starts with not messing around anymore. I'm going to stay away from all people I'm attracted to. Plus, he's the photographer anyway. We're both busy."

"Like that's ever stopped you from having a little bump and grind during slowdowns." She shook her head and walked back toward the setup where food was being plated. "Remember when you almost got us fired for sleeping with the best man at that one wedding?"

I sucked my lips into my mouth before looking away. Laughing would cause her to shove my shoulder and her little ass was strong. I grabbed the dishware and silverware that I'd noted were missing then thrust them at her.

"You should take these out there to the seats that weren't completely set up. The plates are in the far corner and the utensils were two tables over." Eliza stared at me for a moment and I rolled my eyes. "You're worried I'll jump him if I'm around him. Go take care of that and let me get back to work in here."

She nodded. I went about washing my hands and putting my chef's coat back on so I could help the other folks we'd hired to finish setting up the first course.

The night moved from meal to meal smoothly. Each course went out without an issue. People thanked us for the good Southern food and everyone thoroughly enjoyed themselves. By the time the simpler dessert came out, everyone was happy and smiling at everything we'd pulled together. Eliza and two of the other chefs went about starting the clean-up while me and two of the waiters collected plates from the diners.

I'd saved food for all the staff of the event so they could

eat. It was all in a corner of the kitchen. If nothing else, I always wanted those I worked with to know they could eat in between rushes. After some of the places I'd worked while going through school, being hungry while prepping food never sat right with me.

As I got to Rochelle and her groom-to-be, she pulled me to the side for a moment. "Thanks for catering my party, Dez. Everything was delicious. I heard folks talking about wanting to hire you for various events in the near future." She hugged me before kissing my cheek.

I heard the shutter of a camera and turned to see that photographer from earlier, viewfinder to his eye as he snapped a few more photos of me and my friend. She smiled and kept her lips on my face a few seconds longer before pulling back and waving him over.

"Have you met my boo's frat brother?" Rochelle asked.

"We bumped into each other earlier," he said.

"Oh, I see," Rochelle said. "Well, he came over to take our photos for us, and I thought that was the sweetest thing ever."

"Came over from where?" I asked.

Before he could answer me, the shatter of glass sounded behind us. Rushing to see what happened, I found the cake Eliza and I created as a surprise had been knocked over by a drunk guest. There were plates and champagne flutes shattered on the floor beside them.

Somehow, he'd not only stepped on a tablecloth, but he'd also fallen into the cart the cake had been on. I balled my fists and took a deep breath in an attempt to calm myself. Eliza was a foot away as if she'd backed up in horror, staring at the mess on the ground, mouth agape.

"I'm sorry, I didn't see—" The drunk person slurred and hiccuped as he struggled to his feet.

The photographer caught his arm and helped him up before leading him to the closest seat. His eyes met mine.

"Let me help you with this," he said.

"No, it's fine." I waved him off. "We can clean it up. You've got work to do yourself."

Eliza finally regained her composure and turned to the waiter who'd been helping her with the cake.

"Help me find brooms and mops," she said. "Let's try to salvage this disaster."

The two of them walked in the direction of the kitchen. The biggest surprise was lying on the floor. *There is no salvaging that.*

"Rochelle, can you clear the room so we can get this cleaned up?" I asked. "I know folks are still eating, but it would be a helluva lot easier to do this without an audience."

She kissed my cheek. "Thanks for the thought, babes." She and her fiancé started directing people into the other room.

"You didn't have to help." I dropped to my knees beside the photographer. He'd gone about picking up the large pieces of glass and chunks of cake when I wasn't paying attention. "You've got your own stuff to do, you're missing shots I'm sure."

"Nah, I got plenty. I'll snap a few more in a bit if they haven't wrapped up by then, but I'd like it if someone helped me when things like this happened."

I smiled then used a few clean stray napkins to pick up more of the cake. I went to grab a piece of glass, but he placed his hand on mine. "I'll get that. You're shaking," he said. "Don't want you to accidentally cut yourself."

I was so angry, my body had begun vibrating. I hadn't even noticed. I didn't like to show anger because it never solved anything and usually got me into trouble if I did blow up on someone. Growing up, my feelings were swept aside. I quickly learned my emotions had to be masked if I would make it through hard situations, so I buried them.

I took a deep breath and I smiled before thanking him. It was all I could manage. By the time Eliza and the other chef returned, we'd picked up most of the mess. They went about sweeping and mopping up the rest. The photographer offered to help me rinse the cart off and dump the trash outside in the back.

Before we exited the building, I saw a bottle of champagne and grabbed it. *Stress response.* Once we reached the loading dock, I found the hose to rinse down the area while he tossed the trash in the dumpster.

As soon as I squeezed the nozzle on the hose, cake and water splashed back and splattered my chest. I looked down and threw my hands up. The photographer handed me the champagne I'd sat down and directed me to the bench a few feet away.

"Let me take care of this for you. Seems like tonight just isn't as chill as it was supposed to be."

Stressed was a word, but it couldn't begin to describe how I truly felt. I pulled air in through my nostrils and nodded before striding over to take a seat. I drank directly from the bottle as he cleaned up for me. He was so kind, not one complaint about my lack of response to him or even a joke about how it could've been worse. He just helped.

The irritation of this entire debacle was what irked me the most, but here came this sexy-ass man and his seemingly genuine happiness. It was hard to be furious when he was there every step of the way helping without a second thought.

It was almost like he was in my service and I started to want a lot more duty from him. Before I knew it, I'd drank almost the entire bottle of champagne. The photographer took a seat beside me, his chest and pants a little wet.

"How you—" he started, but I interrupted.

"You never told me where you're from," I said.

"I live on the West Coast," he said.

"Good, then breaking my vow tonight won't be so bad."

"What vow?" I sat the near-empty bottle on the ground beside me, stood, and grabbed his hand. He rose to his feet, his frame towering over me as it had done earlier.

"You got a condom?"

"What?" he coughed.

I brought my body flush against his and leaned up on my tip-toes. "I peeped how you've been eyeing me. You saying you hadn't thought about getting it in? You're going back home after this and I'll be here. Call it a parting gift. A thank you. A nice memory."

He cocked his head before a smirk crossed his face. I walked us over to a dark corner at the far end of the empty expanse and pushed him against the wall. His hands flew to my ass as I reached up to bite his lip.

"You with someone?" he asked. "This some spite thing or something?"

"Nope. I like what I like and go after what I want." Those were the last words that came out of either of our mouths before our lips crashed together. Urgent kisses. Heavy breathing. He tasted of peppermint and honey. Likely a drink or a piece of candy. Either way, I wanted more of it.

His lips started traveling down my neck as I unbuttoned his pants and he did the same to my shirt. A rumbling growl sounded in the back of my throat as his teeth found my nipple through the lace bralette I had on.

His tongue flicked the ring through the fabric. My hand wrapped around his shaft. His head banged back against the wall as I worked him out of his jeans and boxer briefs before massaging his length, eliciting a very sexy groan from him.

He flipped us around and pinned my front to the wall,

working my jeans down to my ankles. The cold of the concrete mattered for all of two seconds as heat flooded my entire being. I glanced over my shoulder and saw him drop to his haunches, spreading my legs as far as my pants would allow before his tongue swiped across my folds. I sucked in a breath.

"Wanted to do that the moment I laid my eyes on you," he said.

My muscles tightened and I went to move, not to get away from him, but to get more of this feeling.

As he pulled my hips back, angling my chest further into the wall, I pushed my ass out for him. I worked to open my legs more as the tip of his tongue probed me in the most delicious way. Closing my eyes, I let the feeling wash over me, the warmth heating my core the longer he went. Before I could reach my climax, he stopped and I heard the rip of the condom wrapper.

He tapped his dick against my entrance. He'd stopped but I didn't have time to ask why. A nod over my shoulder was all I could manage before he gave me what I needed so desperately. He bit his lip before pressing into me slowly.

At this point, I didn't want soft, slow strokes. I planted my hands on the wall and started pushing back against him until he was seated deep within me, then we met each other thrust for thrust. The roughness of his jeans rubbed against my bare thighs each time he speared me to the hilt.

My legs started shaking, but I held on because I wanted him to crash over with me. It seemed like I wasn't the only one who needed this quick fuck. One of his hands gripped my waist tight as we kept moving together.

His other covered mine on the wall. Looking toward the ground and bending my knees a bit more, I angled as I continued to slam back against him. His hand slid from my hip up to my breast and he squeezed as he lifted my torso and pushed me flush against the wall.

Our heavy breathing was all I could hear as he pushed in two more times with reckless abandon and I felt myself spill over, him freezing as he followed right behind me. My breathing was ragged, but I couldn't help the smile that formed.

"Well damn," he said, his heart racing against my back as his body held mine up.

I felt like jelly in the best way. I knew I'd broken my vow. I'd have to deal with the internal turmoil later, but right now, I was almost tempted to continue this elsewhere. He smoothed my stray curls from my neck and placed a soft kiss behind my ear before he slid out of me and leaned on the wall beside me.

I blinked a few times. It was strangely nice to have that little moment, but it also told me this couldn't go any further. That was too sweet. I had to work to get my breath under control and pull my jeans up. I needed to get home and clean up soon. Not only was I now sweaty as hell, I had cake on my chest and I'm sure everyone would know I had sex.

I turned around and leaned against the wall, waiting for my legs to feel more stable.

"You should get back before they start wondering where you are," I breathed.

"You good out here?" He asked as he zipped his pants up.

"Yeah, I'll be fine. I'll come in after I grab the cart."

He started buttoning my shirt for me, but I stilled his hands.

"I've got it," I said. "Thanks for the distraction."

"I should be thanking you for the birthday gift."

"It's your birthday?"

He nodded, fighting back a smile.

"You must be really good friends with Rochelle's fiancé."

"Yeah, we were cool in college," he said. "I also wanted to get away. I'll say this made the trip all the better."

"You're welcome," I smirked.

Instead of heading back inside, he waited for me. When we walked back into the dining room, it was empty, but I knew Eliza would know. I couldn't even go a full two weeks without falling into my old habits. At least I got some good dick and this would be one person I wouldn't have to see again.

ALSO BY RAE SHAWN

Chronicles of Cane Series

Cane's Justice

The Unknown Enemy

Ripped Apart

Reaction Chronicles Series

Fatal Reaction

Calculated Reaction

Narcissistic Reaction

Endless Knight Series

Fumble Recovery

Big City, Small World

Uncovering Her Cravings

Standalone

Twelve Days of Thiccmas

For a complete list of my books after this book is published, please
visit my website: www.loveraeshawn.com

www.ingramcontent.com/pod-product-compliance
Lightning Source LLC
Chambersburg PA
CBHW050340030726
47503CB00008B/2540